I0521248

Tears of Heaven

Jewel Adams

Copyright © 2010 Jewel Adams
Jewel of the West Publishing
All Rights Reserved
ISBN-13 978-0615444499
ISBN-10: 0615444490

Library of Congress Control Number: 2011901691

To my husband, Sean.
Life with you has been heaven on earth!
And to Debbie C. The world is a better
place because you are here.

To fly with the wings of an angel
would be a splendid feat,
to experience love's heavenly splendor,
the soul's unparalleled delight!

J.A.

Stockholm, Sweden

Glancing up at the round, metal clock on the wall, I rub my red eyes and sigh deeply. The numbness I'd experienced a few hours earlier is gone now, and in its place is a pain unlike anything I have ever felt in my life. You would think I'd be used to pain, that I would be immune to it. But as I sit in this sterile environment, I realize with agonizing clarity, that I am still human after all. I am still susceptible to the human condition. I can still feel, and it hurts. It hurts something fierce.

I close my eyes for a moment and listen to the rhythmic beep of the monitor as it plays an assuring cadence in my ears. Part of my mind reasons that the steady beep means all is well. The other part is connected to my heart and isn't so sure. And oh, how I wish I could be sure. How I wish I could know for sure that everything will be all right, that my heart, and my soul, haven't been shattered forever. But I guess that is usually where faith comes in. There is no better time for me to learn this than now.

I lift my arms and stretch my aching limbs, the result of remaining in the same position for hours. Then I return my hands to their rightful place–that place being, wrapped around his hand.

My eyes rest on the large corded hand in mine, and I marvel at both the strength and the gentleness of it. I press the back of it against my face, grateful for its warmth. My gaze slowly moves up the lean, muscular arm, taking in the cords of veins trailing up and down beneath lightly tanned skin.

As my eyes move to the smooth, broad chest covered with a thick bandage, I feel the all too familiar burning behind them. Then I gaze up at his face and hot tears once again blur my vision and spill down my cheeks.

I move forward, lifting one of my hands to his face, and gently caress the soft, dark hair lying against his forehead. I slowly trail a finger over his chiseled features, pausing a moment before tracing the outline of his full lips.

Not able to help myself, I lean down and tenderly, softly, gently, press my lips to his. I linger a moment, breathing in the intoxicating and familiar scent of him. Raising up, I smile.

Though he is one hundred percent Russian, to me, Sergei looks like a Greek god. He is beautiful and he is perfect, more perfect than any man I could have ever dreamed of.

But most of all, he is the man I love with all my heart and soul.

The man who's wedding rings I now wear on my finger.

The man I have made an eternal covenant to love forever.

He is the man who has shown me love beyond belief, has healed my once battered heart, and has given me everything.

Now he is lying in this hospital bed fighting for his life because of me.

One

Four months ago.

I examined my reflection in the full-length mirror a final time, sighing deeply at the young woman staring back at me. After a week, the bruises around my left eye and on my right cheek had faded some. Applying some foundation to those areas helped to conceal the spots so no one would notice the signs of what was now a painful part of my past. At least I hoped and prayed it is all in the past.

I smoothed a wrinkle from my peach polo shirt and tucked it into belted khaki trousers. I decided the outfit would work fine for a housekeeper. The only requirement my new employer made as far as a uniform went was that I wore something neat but comfortable. This outfit was both. After applying a little mascara to my lashes and smoothing some clear gloss on my lips, I pulled my long, black hair back into a ponytail and decided I was ready.

As I studied my reflection once more, my thoughts strayed to my parents. Whether he wanted to be or not, my father was responsible for my full lips and black hair. He had inherited his own from his Cuban father and black mother. My mother's Swedish blood provide me with my hazel eyes, which take on a violet hue at times, depending on my mood.

I sighed inward, thinking that it would have been nice if my parents had meant for me to have their features. It would have been nice if they had meant for me to be born at all. I think things definitely would have been different for me if they had.

My mother had been twenty when she moved to the United States from Stockholm to continue her education. She had only been enrolled in South College in Knoxville, Tennessee for a few months when she met Jeff Greenlee. I guess he must have been quite the charmer, because before my mother knew it, she was living with him in a trailer park and pregnant. She didn't even share his name, only his bed.

A week after sharing the supposed blissful news of my eminent arrival with my father, he left home and never came back. Thirteen years later, my mother repeated his Houdini disappearing act by dumping me off on some friends and leaving to find herself. Evidently she must still be looking. It has been eight years and I haven't seen her since.

With both my parents abandoning me, I learned the meaning of rejection early in life. I knew in my soul my mother never wanted me. She'd never shown even an inkling of love toward me. I doubted she even liked me. I was a burden, one that she was anxious to rid herself of.

"What a sad situation!" I remembered people saying. *"What a sad beginning! How will the poor young thing handle life with such a sad beginning? Poor Heaven. Poor, poor thing."*

I shook my head sadly as I thought about my name. *Heaven.* I found out later that the only reason my mother even named me Heaven was because a friend suggested it. I'm surprised she took the suggestion since she had never harbored any warm feelings toward God. If I learned anything when I was with her it was her religious views; she didn't have any.

However, two good things came from her abandonment; the love of a good family and an introduction to the gospel of Jesus Christ. Until moving in with the Copeland family, I had no real knowledge of God and His son. Receiving that knowledge changed my life.

Fastening my watch, I smiled as I thought about Shirley and John Copeland. They were two of the kindest and most loving people I had ever known. They willingly took me into their home, giving me as much love as they did their own two daughters. I couldn't help thinking that God had made a mistake placing me with a mother and father who never wanted me, and that I really should have been born to their family. But I soon realized that God doesn't make mistakes. There had to have been a reason. I wished I knew what that reason was. I wished that I knew the reason for my life, period.

When I turned eighteen I expressed a desire to Shirley to find my mother's family. She and John got the ball rolling, and a couple of weeks later, I had the opportunity to talk to my Swedish grandmother and grandfather for the first time.

Karl and Felicity Gunderson quickly became a part of my life. Gelina, my mother, had been their only child. When she left and eventually broke ties with them, it broke their hearts. They hadn't heard from her in years and didn't know if she was dead or alive. They loved her very much and worried about her a great deal, but they knew their daughter's fate was out of their hands. They still continued to pray that she would contact them one day. It was about all they could do.

I prayed for that as well, but for my grandparents' sake, not mine. Shirley was more of a mother to me than my own mother had ever been, and though I had forgiven her in my heart for leaving, I didn't need her. I sometimes felt a little guilty about my lack of feelings for her, but I couldn't help it. I didn't hate her. I didn't harbor any ill feelings toward her. If I felt anything for her, it was pity for what she missed out on.

I could never understand how my mother could treat her own family that way. And what was even sadder was my mother hadn't even told my grandparents of my existence, which provided me with another painful example of just how much she really cared about me. It was as if I didn't exist. I was their only grandchild and she didn't even have the decency to tell them about me. For this reason, they stayed in close contact with me.

I visited my grandparents a couple of times in Stockholm, and they came to see me in Knoxville. They repeatedly asked me to come and stay with them for a while, and I always gave them the same answer. Someday.

And now, here I was, twenty-one, single, and living with my grandparents.

I straightened the furrow in my brow that appeared whenever I thought of my predicament. *Someday.* It seemed *someday* had come sooner than I'd expected, and under unfortunate circumstances.

I walked over to the window and absently gazed down the cobblestone street. My grandparents lived in Old Town, a charming and bustling section of downtown Stockholm. Their two bedroom apartment was directly over the bakery they owned and operated.

I smiled and closed my eyes as the scent of cakes, croissants, and other European pastries seeped into my room and tickled my senses. I mused that if I wasn't careful, my waistline would expand to the size of Grandma Felicity's, a sure sign of too many samplings of her own recipes.

Looking down the narrow street in either direction, I took in the many outdoor cafes and sidewalk restaurants. Seeing these sights on television travel shows was one thing, but actually living among them was pretty incredible.

I watched various people as they lounged at tables, sipping espresso and indulging in pastries. I noticed as several fair-haired women walked by that clothing in Sweden is very fashionable. Of course, I didn't care for the immodest outfits, but the women donning total body coverage were lovely.

I had always considered myself a very modest person. Even before being baptized into the Mormon church, I never indulged in tank tops, short shorts, or plunging necklines. Despite my mother's lack of standards, I did have mine, and I wasn't willing to compromise them. That was one of the things Ross said he loved about me . . .

I turned away from the window and sighed, sitting down on the wooden chair by my bed. *Ross.* I could never escape my thoughts or memories of him. With time, I prayed that I would. After all, he was the reason I'd had to leave the states. He was the reason I felt that my heart would be permanently closed.

And I continued to pray that, just like the bruises, the painful memories of him would soon begin to fade.

I was nineteen when I first started dating Ross Townsend. He had moved to Knoxville from Toronto, Canada, and had rented an apartment five minutes away from the complex in which I lived. I was an assistant manager at a department store in the mall, and he was working construction on a building across the street. He came into the store one day on his lunch break to buy a dress shirt and a pair of slacks for a dinner party he was planning to attend that night.

All it took was one smile and I was done in, completely taken with his blond-haired, blue-eyed surfer-boy looks. Evidently, he was pleased with me as well. We ended up going out that night, and every other night through the following weeks.

I learned that Ross was an only child from a very affluent family. His father was a doctor, his mother, a fashion designer. His parents still lived in Toronto but did travel to the states occasionally. The way Ross talked about his parents told me he looked up to them a great deal. In a way, I thought they sounded a little too perfect, but it only validated to me how much he loved them, which made me like him all the more. I envied the contentment that he experienced in his relationship with his parents. Somehow, things always seemed to come up and I never got the chance to meet them.

I thought Ross was wonderful. He did and said exactly the right things, and he could charm the heart of even the coldest of women. To me, he was amazing. He made me feel wanted and accepted.

I had never been in a relationship before, so I had nothing to compare it to. I was so inexperienced when it came to matters of the heart, and I thought everything was going as it should between us. John and Shirley also thought he was wonderful and frequently asked me to bring him over for dinner.

To my girlfriends, Ross was every woman's dream guy, every woman's fantasy. And he was.

Every woman that is, except for me.

Unfortunately, by the time I discovered he wasn't my dream guy, it was too late, for he had become my nightmare.

It began to happen slowly. Subtly.

At first it was just little things. Ross thought it would be better if I wore my hair up in a bun when I went to work. He told me it looked more professional and would attract less attention. I respected his opinion, so I took his advice.

Then he told me pantsuits would be more professional than the casual dresses and floral skirts I wore. These two things should have been my first clue that something was wrong, but as I said, this was the first time I'd ever had a boyfriend.

Soon, there were other things. If Ross stopped by the store to see me and found me helping a male customer, I would get the silent treatment for a couple of days. Then he would apologize and tell me he knew I was just doing my job.

If a waiter paid me a little too much attention when we went out together, it was my fault, and again I would get the silent treatment but no apology, as if I'd done something to encourage the attention.

At times when he would call my apartment and I wasn't there, he automatically assumed I was with someone else, and the harder I tried to prove to him that he was the only man in my life, the more jealous he became. I wore myself out feeling guilty about things I had no control over. And the more worn I became, the more my feelings for him began to fade.

Soon after, the pain began.

On the one year anniversary of our first date together, we went out to celebrate. We dined at one of the nicest Japanese restaurants in Knoxville. I had never been the place before, but I had heard that the chefs there put on quite a show, so I had been excited about going.

Throughout dinner, Ross was so pleasant and thoughtful, and I smiled the entire time, my heart suddenly filled with hope for us.

After dinner, Ross said he wanted to take me dancing. I told him I wasn't comfortable going. He wanted to know why.

I looked at him and thought, *Because so far, this night has been perfect. If we go dancing, it won't be perfect anymore because you will find some reason to fly into a jealous rage.* Instead of bravely fessing up, I smiled and gave in. I mean, he was trying. I figured I could at least give him the benefit of the doubt. It had been a good evening so far.

Returning my mind to the present for a moment, I leaned forward and rubbed my temples, a familiar tension building inside me as I again relived that night. I remembered every single second of it, as if it had just happened.

The ride home had been silent. Ross wouldn't even look at me. Of course, I was too naive to realize I was sitting next to a ticking bomb. If I had known, I would have tried harder to find a way to defuse it. When we reached my apartment, he walked me to the door and asked if he could come in for a few minutes. Like normal, I said sure.

Once we were inside and I closed the door, he began pacing back and forth. Occasionally he would stop, look at me, then begin pacing again. It was almost like watching a caged animal. Finally, I walked over to him, took his hand in mine, and asked him what was wrong. Since I was wearing three inch heels, my five-feet-seven inch height was elevated slightly and put me almost eye to eye with him. He wasn't a very tall guy.

He looked at me, the muscles in his jaw twitching slightly. "You really shouldn't draw so much attention to yourself, you know that?"

The statement had rendered me speechless. *Whoa! Where in the world did that come from?* I wondered. I managed to smile and moved closer. "The only attention I try to draw these days is yours."

Ross pulled his hand away abruptly and said, "Well, you sure have a hell of a way of showing it!"

I closed my eyes and took a deep breath. Suddenly, I had had enough. I hadn't known that this wasn't the smartest moment to come to that conclusion, but I was tired. I was tired of giving and giving in our relationship and coming up empty. I sighed and looked into his eyes sadly.

"Ross, I care for you a great deal, but I can't do this anymore."

He glared at me with those piercing blue eyes. "What do you mean?" he asked, an increase of anger showing in his expression. "You want to break up with me?"

Then before I had the chance to respond or even think, the back of his hand landed hard against my face.

I was completely stunned. I immediately pressed my hand to my throbbing cheek, a menagerie of emotions flowing through my mind and heart as tears quickly filled my eyes. When they began to trickle down my cheeks, the hardness in Ross' eyes completely diminished, and in its place was a look of remorse.

When he moved closer to me, I flinched, afraid he would hit me again. Surprisingly, I saw his eyes fill with tears. He began expressing his sorrow over what he had done. He said he didn't know what had come over him and that he had been so afraid of losing me, he'd lost it. He continued to apologize profusely and promised me it would never happen again. He promised that things would be different from now on, that *he* would be different.

And like a fool, I believed him and gave him another chance. Why I did it, I'll never know. I guess I thought there was still hope for us. I had to at least try.

Looking back now, I think deep down, I was trying to prove to Ross I was worth loving, and having his love was worth whatever I had to endure. I could take the pain if it meant not being alone. At least *he* wanted me. What a misguided soul I was.

I was never one to be a glutton for punishment, but six months later, I began to learn with certainty that abuse never stops with the first hit or slap, and there is almost always a second time.

As time passed, I slowly began to be comfortable in our relationship again and was even considering marrying Ross, thinking he really had changed. He had become so attentive and loving to me, making me feel like I was the most important thing in his life. I thought things would go on that way. But I was wrong. All it took was one hug given to me by a male co-worker at a party to set the ticking bomb off once again.

And thus, the cycle had begun; a continuous pattern of abuse, then apology, only now stalking had been added to the mix. I had become so afraid of him, I didn't know which way to turn. Yet I was afraid of losing him too, so I never told anyone what was happening. I kept everything hidden away inside, hoping that someday he would change.

I managed to avoid John and Shirley whenever the bruises were too visible to cover up. I even called in sick to work a few times. I had practically altered my life and myself to the point that I didn't even recognize *me* anymore.

I couldn't eat, so I lost weight.

I couldn't sleep, so there were permanent dark circles under my eyes.

I had become afraid of my own shadow.

I was an utter mess, feeling completely trapped in a hopeless situation and afraid to try and do anything about it.

"Poor Heaven! Poor child!" The voices of my youth had begun to visit me frequently.

Then came the straw that finally broke this camel's back.

I had come home one night after going out with a girlfriend and found Ross sitting in his car in front of my apartment waiting for me. I don't know why I felt I owed him an explanation, but I did. I started to tell him where I had been, but before I could even get a word out, he got out of the car, took my arm, pulled me into the apartment, and laid into me.

This time, however, there was not the usual apology at the sight of my tears afterwards. But he did leave me with a suggestion.

"Listen, baby," he said softly, pulling my hand away from my swollen eye and forcing me to look at him. "There's only one way you can prove your love to me now. And you know what way that is." He smiled at my astonished expression and added, "I think I have waited long enough. I suggest you make an appointment at the clinic and take care of yourself . . . because I *will* finally have what's mine."

I stood looking at him with frightened incredulity. Ross wasn't Mormon, but he knew I was. He also knew where I stood when it came to the subject of intimacy, and he had never attempted to cross that line. Suddenly he was ready to enforce a change of those rules, one that I had no intention of letting him enforce.

When I said nothing, he added, "And don't even think about running, because I *will* find you."

I felt my eyes grow large. I remained fearfully silent and he smiled again. Then he kissed my bruised cheek and left.

That night, after explaining everything to John and Shirley, who both shed angry tears over the whole situation, I began to pack. I had already lost my self-esteem and my trust in men. I had even lost faith in my own judgment. My virtue was the only thing I had left that belonged to me, and I wasn't about to let Ross take that the way he had taken everything else—the way I had *allowed* him to take everything else.

Beginning to formulate a plan, I picked up a flower pot that had been knocked over and set it back on the table. As I knelt down and began cleaning up the dirt, I paused a moment, holding a handful of dirt. I made a fist and watched it as it slowly crumbled through my fingers.

And so goes my life, I mused tearfully. *It's falling apart and slipping right through my fingers.*

"Poor, poor child!" The voices were back again.

I angrily brushed the tears away from my sore face. "No more '*Poor Heaven*,'" I declared. "No more."

I knew I had to leave, but where could I go that he wouldn't come after me?

The next morning I called my grandparents, cleaned out my bank accounts, and left.

Pulling my thoughts forward, I sighed. *And here I am.*

I checked the time and decided I had better put away the painful memories and get going. I was beginning a new life now. A safe life. Hopefully. It wouldn't do to be late my first day on the job.

Heading to the door, my eyes fell on a small framed

picture of my mother that sat on a wicker chest. The picture was taken in front of the Royal Palace. With her pale-blond hair, hazel eyes, and ballerina figure, she was stunning. I supposed my grandparents placed the picture there thinking I would probably want some tangible memory of my mother.

Nothing could be further from the truth.

I shook my head as I closed the door. *Poor Gelina. Poor, poor Gelina.*

Walking through the bakery, I couldn't help but smile as I watched my grandparents put an order together for a customer. If I'd had more time, I would have hung around the bakery for a while and kept them company. But I knew stalling for time was not an option, which is really what I would have been doing.

Truthfully, I was still a little nervous about meeting my new employer. My grandmother had arranged the job for me a couple of days after I arrived. She and my grandfather had become acquainted with the man last year when he began to be a frequent customer in their bakery Since I'd only been in Stockholm for a week, I hadn't had a chance to meet him.

Grandma Felicity told me Sergei Petrenko was a retired hockey player from Russia. He spend a year in the US. before making his home in Stockholm. Grandma described him as a quiet man who enjoyed his solitude, something I could definitely understand and relate to. I guarded my privacy as well, so I figured we would get along great. Besides, I was going there to do a job, not socialize.

Two

Riding the bus through downtown Stockholm was an interesting experience. I found myself casually glancing at the faces of various passengers seated around me. Just as in America, the people here were all so different. Since I've always been a people watcher, I found myself trying to read a few expressions, but none of them were discernible.

I looked toward the front of the bus and noticed a man who appeared to be staring at me. Maybe he was staring through me, I don't know. But it unnerved me. I can't say for certain why it did. I had an idea, though, and that bothered me as well.

Looking back, I could see that Ross had taken more from

me than I realized, and I had no clue how to get it back, or even if I wanted it back. The wall I managed to build around me kept me safe, and I knew that safety mechanism would probably forever be ingrained in me. For now, I was okay with that.

I sighed. Truthfully, I think a part of me was missing from the moment I drew my first breath at birth, and I was never allowed to find that part. As I grew, I became too busy looking out for myself to truly know there was more to life than what I saw in the little world I was being brought up in.

Glimpsing into the worlds of other children my age, I had witnessed love, laughter, respect, and family. I honestly couldn't remember experiencing one moment of love or anything closely resembling it from my mother. I learned early that I could never depend on her for anything, not even love.

It was true, what people used to say. *What a sad beginning I had in life.*

Pulling my thoughts forward, I glanced down at the pant leg of a teenage boy sitting next to me. There was a small rip in the knee of his jeans. I knew some considered this a fashion statement, but for me, it brought back memories of a time when a rip in my clothes was a detriment.

I was only six when my mother began to harp about how much it was costing her to keep me clothed. At that age, rips and tears were supposed to be normal. It was also supposed to be normal for a parent to try and repair their children's clothing, but I could never use the word *normal* to describe my mother in any way.

She determined that since I was the one who had ripped my clothes, I should be responsible for fixing them. So, at six and a half years old, I taught myself how to repair my clothes.

I sighed, slightly shaking my head at the memory. At least I learned to take care of myself early. I learned a lot of things early. Thank goodness the Copeland family came into my life and taught me to love, but now *that* even scared me, and it made me more determined than ever to guard my heart.

Keeping my thoughts in the present, I looked toward the head of the bus once more. Still finding the man's eyes on me, I turned my attention to the passing scenery and kept it there until I reached my stop.

Following the directions my grandmother had given me, I found Mr. Petrenko's home with little difficulty. I knocked on the large double doors, both marveling at and dreading the size of the beautiful home.

The house was a large, country French design with sunset yellow stucco, white shutters and trim, and a red tiled roof. Taking in the large, granite water fountain out front, as well as the rest of the amazing landscaping, I could definitely picture the house featured in an issue of *Better Homes and Gardens*. Everything about it was grand.

I knocked once more, a little harder this time. After another moment, the door opened and I found myself staring up into the light brown eyes of Sergei Petrenko. I was a little startled but recovered quickly. I hadn't expected him to answer the door himself. With a house this extravagant, I expected him to have a butler. I cleared my throat nervously and introduced myself.

"I'm Heaven Gunderson," I said, extending my hand.

"It is a pleasure to meet you, Heaven," he said with a smile, the gentle, deep tone of his voice softening his thick Russian accent. He squeezed my hand gently. "Come in, please," he added, moving aside.

"Thank you."

After letting my eyes roam around the foyer for a moment, I was suddenly ready to jump right into my duties. Now that the official moment of meeting him was over, I felt slightly more relaxed, grateful that he seemed friendly enough.

He showed me where I could store my purse and sweater, then he gave me a quick tour of the house. It truly was beautiful, even more so than I imagined. On the main floor, there was the formal living and dining room, a library, family room, and a huge kitchen. On the second level, there were four bedrooms, two bathrooms, and a laundry room. The top floor consisted of two more bedrooms, including an enormous master suite, each with its own private bath. There was an exercise room and a theater room as well.

Taking everything in, I knew I would have my work cut out for me. But then again I figured that since he lived there alone, it wouldn't be too hard to keep on top of everything.

While I was pondering this, Mr. Petrenko asked, "Do you think you can handle the job or is it going to be too much?"

I was slightly annoyed, both at him and myself. At myself for allowing my thoughts to show on my face, and at him for assuming I couldn't handle a house this size. But not wanting to jump to conclusions and judge him too harshly, I swallowed my pride and said in what I hoped was an assuring voice, "I can handle the job just fine, Mr. Pertrenko." When he again smiled and nodded, I was grateful that I had swallowed my pride. "Would you like me to start anywhere specific?" I asked.

"No," he said softly, staring into my eyes and unnerving me. "You can start anywhere you want and make up your own routine, but I do have one request for you, though."

"Yes?" I questioned warily.

"I know I am your employer, but no more Mr. Petrenko, all right? My name is Sergei."

I stood quietly for a moment, staring up into his eyes, not knowing what to say. He continued to look at me expectantly and I soon found my voice. "Fine," I said, finally pulling my eyes away from his. "I will get started, then."

He smiled again and started away from me, calling over his shoulder, "I have to step out for a few moments. I will not be gone long."

"All right," I said softly, still glued to the same spot. I watched his tall retreating form until he turned the corner and was no longer in sight. I stood for another moment and silently wondered what I had gotten myself into. My new employer wasn't at all what I had expected. With his tall, lean-muscled physique, dark tousled hair, and warm brown eyes, he was too handsome, too beautiful, and too perfect for words.

And he was a danger to be avoided.

After another moment, I finally got my feet moving and started my duties. I had never been a housekeeper before, but I found myself enjoying the job. I figured that as long as my employer didn't have any riotous parties or suddenly have more people running in and out of his house, it would be pretty easy to keep up with everything. If that changed in the future, it would be harder, but I would still do my job.

I found that each room I entered and every item I lifted to clean or dust brought questions to my mind about my employer. I couldn't help wondering why Mr. Pet . . . why Sergei picked that particular thing and what kind of sentimental value he placed on it.

Like the porcelain figurine sitting on the dresser in his bedroom. It was of an angel with her hands resting on the shoulders of a young boy. Or the small painting that hung on a wall in the theater room. It was a picture of a family picnicking beneath a large tree. These aren't the kinds of things I expected to find in the home of a single, retired sports jock. Pictures and figurines of immodestly dressed women or sports photos, maybe, but not these things.

I finally brushed the questions aside, reminding myself it was none of my business why he picked these things, and that I was only there to do a job.

I kept my mind in that mode of thinking throughout the day and it helped to keep the mental questions at bay. But when I finally hauled the vacuum cleaner into the family room, the last room I needed to clean, my eyes did a double-take as they landed on the large, framed photo of the Stockholm LDS Temple, which was hanging on the wall to the left. I had only given the room a brief glance earlier, otherwise I would have noticed it.

I absently dropped the cleaning rag as I slowly approached the picture. I hadn't had the chance to actually see the beautiful temple yet, but I did recognize it. A woman in my ward back in Knoxville had given me a book of temples around the world, and for some reason I had always favored the Stockholm, Sweden Temple. Maybe it was the Swedish blood in me, an internal feeling of kinship with any and all things Swedish.

Still, it was a beautiful temple. I had read somewhere that the land on which the temple is built was originally the site of an ancient Viking temple. There was even supposed to be a Viking burial ground about a mile away from the temple site. I found that information incredible.

But why would he have a photo of a temple? I wondered. My eyes took in the picture of the Savior hanging just to the right of it. Suddenly aware of my heartbeat speeding up, I pressed a hand to my chest.

He couldn't be!

Hearing a quiet movement behind me, I turned around and was briefly startled as I again found myself looking up into the hypnotic gaze of Sergei.

"It is beautiful, is it not?" he asked softly.

At the moment I could only nod. Finally finding my voice once more, I asked, "Are you LDS?"

His eyes showed pleasant surprise. "I am," he answered.

"So am I," I said softly.

He smiled at me then, as if he had suddenly discovered an old friend. "Small world, is it not?"

"It is," I said back, giving him a timid smile in return. When he continued to stand there looking at me with those searching brown eyes, I began to be nervous, and I didn't like that feeling at all. "Excuse me," I said, moving around him and picking up the rag I had dropped.

"I just need to do this room and I will be done for the day." I bravely looked at him again. "Unless you need me to do something else."

"No," he said softly. "Everything looks great. Thank you."

I heaved a small sigh of relief, having worried that he wouldn't find my work satisfactory. "You're welcome. And thank you for giving me this job. I appreciate it very much."

"It was my pleasure. Your grandparents speak very highly of you."

"Thanks," I mumbled again, suddenly wondering how much Grandma and Grandpa really told him about me. When I said nothing else, he smiled once more and left me to finish, which I did as quickly as possible. The last thing I wanted to do was become more familiar with Sergei. I didn't want to know anything about him that wasn't related to my job, and I didn't want him to know my private business, either.

After I finished, I put the vacuum and the cleaning supplies away. I walked through the massive house a final time to make sure I hadn't forgotten anything. Satisfied that I hadn't, I went in search of my employer.

I found Sergei standing in kitchen with a glass of lemonade in his hand, gazing out the large window down into the backyard. Having had to pull my own eyes away from the view earlier, I understood why he was so captivated. It was absolutely breathtaking.

The grass was lush and green, and there were gloriously colored pansies and poppies lining a cobblestone walkway leading out to a beautiful, white iron gazebo. A half a mile in the distance lay the harbor, filled with various sizes and types of boats. The sunlight shimmered against the water like glittering jewels, and waves gently rolled inward. I sighed, thinking it had to be one of the most lovely and romantic views I had ever seen.

My eyes moved to Sergei again. His stance was relaxed, as if he didn't have a care in the world. He even radiated peace.

What would that be like . . .

Reining in my thoughts, I approached my employer. He turned as I neared.

"Would you like a glass of lemonade?" he asked.

" No, thank you. I'm all done if you want to check everything once more."

He smiled. "I do not need to check. I am sure it is fine. Thank you for everything." He picked up an envelope lying on the counter and handed it to me.

I thanked him and said, "I'll see you next week." Then I turned to go.

"Let me walk you to the door." He set his glass on the

counter.

"You really don't have to," I insisted.

"I know," he said softly.

Saying nothing more, he moved behind me and followed me to the door. Hearing his footsteps on the tile floor behind mine, I wondered why it was suddenly harder for me to breathe. He moved forward and opened the door. I turned to him.

"Thank you again for the job."

"You are very welcome. I am glad to have you here. And if anything should ever come up and you need to switch days, just call me."

"I will."

Walking away, I listened for the closing of the door but didn't hear it, and I knew he was watching me. I could feel his gaze and it was unsettling. I had also felt it during the times I was working in the same room he occupied, but I chose to ignore him. Once or twice when I did glance at him, he looked at me intently and smiled. Then he turned his attention to other things. His presence definitely did things to my nerves.

I shook my head slightly, putting Sergei out of my thoughts and pressed for home.

Three

I spent the rest of that week and the next sightseeing.

Since my grandparents had to run the bakery, I went alone. I didn't really mind it though. I was able to take my time and spend as long as I wanted and not have to worry about tiring them out.

Walking through town, I stopped many times and took pictures of old churches. I toured each one, admiring their gold and brass ornate interiors, the dark woods and various colors of marble taking my breath away.

I also took countless photos of the Royal Castle. The gray stone walls of the palace loomed above me, casting a shadow over the entire block. The enormous building was only one of ten royal palaces in Sweden. Why the family would need ten I'll never know, but I felt sure the other nine were just as beautiful. After snapping a few close up shots of the guards, I did a little shopping. I purchased a couple of fashionable, yet modest outfits, and I bought a few things to send to the Copeland family.

On one day I went to a place called *Skansen*. It was a large, open air museum. In many parts of the place there were old cabins in which workers depicted how the Swedish people once lived. I loved touring the bakery, the glass blowing and wood shops, as well as the machine shop and the old mercantile store. There was even a zoo and an amusement park. It was an incredible place with a lot of history.

After walking around for a while, I stopped on a wooden bridge to rest. Leaning against the railing and staring out over the large pond, I closed my eyes and enjoyed the soft breeze that gently lifted my hair and cooled my hot skin. As I relished the comfortable sensation, my mind began to wander.

This would be a great place to bring a family, if I had one, that is. The intruding thought unnerved me, but watching the smiling faces of children with their parents and listening to their laughing voices, it was hard not to wonder what it would be like to have a family of my own.

Though, if I were really being honest with myself, my

background would make me one of the last people who should have a family. I didn't think I had anything to give to a child, or for that matter even a husband. I wished that I did. My life was too unstable, too uncertain. I was an emotional mess, pure and simple, and one little thing might throw me over the edge, bringing an end to what sanity I had left.

Deep inside, however, there was a part of me that longed to have a family of my own, but I didn't think it was in the cards for me. And I didn't think it ever would be.

I silently scolded myself. These self-inflicted mind games were pointless, and I knew it. Why did I keep doing it to myself? If the past had taught me anything, it was that some things were not meant to be.

Closing my eyes and taking a deep breath, I shook my head and turned my thoughts elsewhere.

That same evening I decided to take a Viking boat tour, which included dinner. The massive boat was an impressive replica of one of the enormous old wooden ships. I spent almost a half an hour before I boarded just taking pictures of it.

Once the tour started, we sailed for two hours around the harbor, dining on wooden platters of roast beef, chicken, fish, and vegetables. Dessert was a large piece of spiced apple cake with sauce and berries.

I thoroughly enjoyed feasting on the delicious dinner while taking in the view of the lovely homes and old buildings along the shore. I found myself listening to the tourists as they talked excitedly and snapped pictures left and right. The scenery really was incredible. I mused that if I was gifted in poetry, I could put the picture into words, but even then, I don't know if they would do the view before my eyes justice.

At one point during the tour, I could even make out Sergei's large home in the distance. It was even more breathtaking from the harbor. Against my will, I smiled, doing my best to fight the warm feeling that immediately entered me at the sight of it. I could almost picture him standing at the kitchen window gazing out at the passing boats. Maybe he could even see the boat I was on. My smile widened. An old viking boat would be hard to miss. My warmth increased.

"No, no, no!" I mumbled under my breath, taking control of my mind.

Turning my head and focusing my eyes elsewhere, I managed to squelch the warm feeling quickly. I didn't want to think about my employer today. As it was, I had already given him more thought than I'd wanted to because of the questions Grandma Felicity bombarded me with the first night I had gotten home from work two weeks before. When I finally went back to Sergei's the following Monday to clean, I had to fight to keep my thoughts from straying to him as I worked. And when we were in the same room, it took everything in me to keep my eyes from moving to him.

He was truly a beautiful man. It was hard not to admire the way his neatly pressed shirt fit over his broad, muscular shoulders, or the way it tucked into his belted slacks, which only accentuated his narrow yet masculine waist. I smiled whenever his handsome brow furrowed during the times he was deep in thought, the way he'd press a hand into his hair and stand with a look of puzzlement on his face when he was looking for something he'd misplaced. And I liked the way his eyes lit up when he finally found what he was searching for.

I wasn't supposed to notice these things. I didn't want to, and each and every time I had to exert the effort to pull my eyes and my thoughts away from him, I screamed inwardly and mentally blamed my weakness on my grandmother.

Rubbing a hand over my face, I took a deep breath and willed away the frown that accompanied the memory of my fifty question evening with my grandmother, which was, even now, the catalyst of my thoughts.

"Well, what was he like, dear?" Grandma asked.

"He was nice," I answered.

Grandma tried again. "Well, how was it to work for him? I mean, did you talk about anything? Did you get to know him or learn any more about him?"

I sighed and tried not to be annoyed. "He's nice to work for, *Farmor*." I had begun to use the Swedish word for grandmother more and more because I liked the way it sounded. "And no, I didn't ask him anything about himself."

"Nothing?" Grandma said, appalled.

Give it a rest, Grandma! I knew what she was getting at and where this was going. She was fine-tuning her Yenta skills. "Okay, I found out we are of the same faith," I said, hoping that would satisfy her for a while.

"You mean he's a Mormon, too?" she asked, her eyebrows raised.

"Yes, *Farmor*," I said with an almost impatient sigh.

"Hmmm," she said, becoming quiet for a moment. I couldn't help wondering what she was thinking. She and my grandfather were Catholic and had no interests in changing their religion, but they respected my beliefs and never tried to change them. This was one of the many things I loved about them.

After another moment, Grandma looked up at me and softly said, "Small world, *ja?*"

I managed a smile as I remembered Sergei saying the same thing. "*Ja, Farmor*, it is a small world." Then thinking that was the end of it, I stood to leave the room, but Grandpa Karl put a gentle hand on my arm to stop me.

I stood quietly waiting for him to fire his round of

questions at me, but he didn't. Instead he took my face in his hands and pressed a kiss to my forehead. Pulling back and looking into my eyes, he said, "I know you have had a tough time of it, but you have to stop being afraid. You need to try and let the past go and learn to trust again." He caressed my face and smiled. "You have to open your heart again. God cannot perform His work in it until you do."

I smiled tearfully at his soft-spoken bluntness. "I don't want God to perform *that* kind of work in me right now, *Farfar*. I'm not ready, and I don't know if I will ever be."

Grandpa kissed my forehead once more and whispered, "But God knows what is best for us." He said nothing more and the subject was dropped, or so I thought. As I was leaving the kitchen to go to my room, I overheard my grandfather tell my grandmother softly, "God will bless her with what is best."

Pulling my thoughts forward as the ship brought us back to our starting point, I found myself apologizing to God for my closed heart, and I prayed that He understood. Deep down, I knew He did. I had no idea, however, as I stepped off the ship and headed home, how truthful my grandfather's final words that night were.

I would soon find out.

Four

The following Monday I asked Sergei if it would be okay if I cut a few of the tulips in the courtyard and brought them inside and he heartily gave me permission. I put the beautiful red flowers in a crystal vase and placed it in the library to give the room a little more color. I smiled at the effect, having a flashback of the movie, *The Remains of the Day*. The thought made me smile wider.

"They look beautiful."

Sergei's voice startled me. I turned to him slightly but kept my eyes fixed on the flowers. "They do brighten the room."

"I think the house just needed a woman's touch."

"I'm glad you are pleased." His comment had been unexpected and I did my best to appear unaffected . . . but I was. Feeling his eyes on me, I said, "I'll go and start on the family room and get out of your way."

"You are never in the way, Heaven." He smiled. "I am glad to have you here."

Not knowing how to respond, I just nodded and left the library. I had to get out of there and the sooner I finished, the sooner I could leave.

I quickly vacuumed and dusted. I changed the bag in the wastepaper basket, fluffed the pillows on the small sofa, and cleaned the glass table sitting next to it.

I felt his presence before he even spoke.

"I have something for you, Heaven."

I sighed inwardly and turned around. Sergei was holding a flat square package wrapped in brown paper.

"What is it?" I asked warily.

"It is something I picked up for you over the weekend."

What is this? "You really shouldn't have." What I actually meant was *I really wish you wouldn't have. Why did you? And what do you want?*

Seeming to read my thoughts through my expression, Sergei sighed, the expression on his handsome face changing to one I couldn't read. Sadness, disappointment, exasperation maybe. I couldn't tell.

"Heaven, because I want to do something nice for you does not mean I expect something in return. I simply saw this and wanted you to have it."

Feeling ashamed for my thoughts, I said, "I'm sorry." When was I going to get it through my head that every man I meet was not Ross? I forced a smile.

That familiar gorgeous smile slowly spread across his face again. "You are forgiven." He handed me the gift.

"Thank you," I said, accepting it.

Sergei stood and watched me open it and I tried to keep my hands from shaking under his gaze. I pulled the paper away and gasped softly as my eyes fell on the beautifully framed painting of the Stockholm Temple.

He came closer. "I thought maybe you could hang it in your room."

"It is beautiful," I whispered. I finally looked up at him and smiled, genuinely smiled for the first time in a long time. "Thank you."

"You are welcome," he said and my heart warmed at the pleasure his face expressed. "I am glad you like it." He sobered. "I will leave you to finish, then." He turned to go.

Feeling like a total idiot for making such a big deal over his giving me the gift in the first place, I quickly touched his arm and said, "Sergei, thank you again. I love it."

He smiled warmly. "You are most welcome."

When I arrived home, I took the painting to my room and hung it above the head of my bed, then I stood staring at it for a moment. The artist's rendering of the beautiful temple was incredible, and the colors were so vivid. It made me long to go there more now than ever.

I truly was grateful for the gift. More so because nothing had been expected in return. And I knew now that Sergei would ask for nothing.

It was very thoughtful of him.

Five

That Sunday while my grandparents attended mass, I attended the Stockholm ward for the first time. I had called the night before and asked for directions. My grandparents agreed to let me use their car because their own church was within walking distance. I thoroughly enjoyed driving the little red Peugeot through the city, easily maneuvering it through the erratic European traffic. I especially appreciated the fact that, just as in America, the Swedes drove on the right side of the road.

Despite a couple of wrong turns, I made it to sacrament meeting on time and I was pleased with myself for the accomplishment.

The members were warm and friendly, and many of them spoke a little English. I was made to feel very welcome. Thankfully, English translation was available for sacrament meeting and I was able to enjoy it more. So far I had only learned a few words in Swedish, but I was determined to learn how to communicate well within the next couple of months.

Despite feeling like I was coming down with something, I thoroughly enjoyed the meetings and looked forward to getting to know the members. I did, however, find myself looking for Sergei's face in the crowd. Then I remembered that he'd left a message with my grandparents the day before, informing me that he would be out of town for the weekend. He wouldn't be back until Monday night. He said he would leave the key for me under the mat in front of the back patio door.

I hated the part of me that felt slightly disappointed he wouldn't be there, and I tried to convince myself that it didn't matter. It wasn't supposed to matter because Sergei was my employer and nothing more. I wanted nothing more.

But that night as I sunk beneath the fluffy down comforter, my final thoughts were on Sergei and his absence. Again, I felt disappointed, but I figured at least there would be no distractions.

Six

I awakened the next morning feeling terrible. My throat and body ached, and it seemed to get worse as the day wore on. For this reason, it took me a little longer than it should have to get all of the cleaning done. Still, I pushed myself and managed to take care of everything. I didn't want Sergei to come home and find my work incomplete. The house usually stayed so clean, I almost doubted that he would have noticed. But I would have known. So in a way, I really was glad he wasn't there.

On the crowded bus heading home, I rested my head against the wall, praying that I wouldn't miss my stop. I felt so terrible and my head ached so much, it hurt to even focus. It took everything to keep from sliding off the seat.

By the time I finally got home, I was completely worn out. I had no energy and it was painful to even move. Grandma suggested that I go straight to bed and I immediately complied, wanting to get over whatever I had quickly so I would be well enough to work the following week.

I changed into a light cotton nightshirt and climbed into bed. Turning my head slightly, I tried to focus on the view of the sky through my window. My eyes took in the gathering clouds, which were evidence of a pending rainstorm. I found myself praying that Sergei would make it back safely.

Feeling the ache in my head growing even more prominent, I finally closed my heavy eyelids and gave in to the beckoning darkness.

I didn't know how long I had been asleep, but I slowly awakened to the feel of a gentle hand pressing softly against my cheek. Keeping my eyes closed, I relished the comfort it gave. After another moment I finally opened my eyes slightly to see Sergei's blurry image. Then I closed them and thought, *Great, now I'm dreaming about the man.* I opened them again and blinked a few times to clear my vision. As his face became clear, I realized I wasn't dreaming.

I managed to ask hoarsely, "What are you doing here?"

"I was worried about you," he answered softly, his hand still pressed to my face.

Doing my best to ignore the feel of his gentle caress, I asked, "How did you know?"

He smiled that beautiful smile, the one that was now becoming so familiar to me. "When I arrived home and saw your paycheck on the counter, I was concerned. So I called Felicity and she told me you were sick."

"I guess I felt so awful, I forgot it." Thinking about what a sight I must be, I added, "But you didn't have to come all the way here to bring it."

Squeezing my hand with his free one, he said, "I did not come just to bring you the check. I came to make sure you are all right."

Again trying my best to not react to his nearness I said, "I'll be fine." As if my body was trying to prove me wrong, I suddenly began to have chills, which Sergei immediately noticed.

He released my hand and pulled the comforter up over me. I turned to my side, vaguely aware of him gently tucking it around me. He leaned closer, pressed a hand to my forehead, and said I was very warm. Hearing the concern in his voice and having him so close brought an extra warmth to my insides that

47

had nothing to do with my illness.

Sergei must have left briefly, because the next thing I knew, he was urging me to drink some herbal tea, crooning softly to me in Russian. I was so weak, it took a great deal of effort to sit up enough to drink it. I couldn't remember ever being so sick before.

I pushed the cup away a little, but Sergei held it to my lips and softly said, "Try to take a little more." I took another small sip.

After helping me lie back down and tucking the comforter around me once more, he asked me if he could get me anything else.

Looking up into his soulful, light brown eyes, I wondered why he had come, and why he stayed. He didn't even know me. I was his employee, yet the concern he was showing toward me was that of someone he'd known forever. In answer to his question, I finally shook my head no and whispered, "Thank you."

Seven

I slept through the next couple of days, waking every now and then to take some flu medicine Grandpa had purchased. Occasionally I heard muffled voices, and despite the fog clouding my thoughts, I was sure I recognized Sergei's gentle voice among them. I felt very comforted.

By Thursday I was feeling a little better and managed to get up and shower, but I spent most of the day lying on the living room sofa under a light blanket. I still felt a little weak, but at least I was out of the bedroom.

I was able to watch a little television, when I wasn't dozing off, that is. Of course, even when I was awake, there really wasn't much on to watch.

I discovered that the Swedes really liked American television shows. Half the shows that were on were American with Swedish overdubbing. Watching them reminded me of watching Asian movies in America with English overdubbing. At another time it would have been amusing. I decided that lounging around with nothing to do was highly overrated and I vowed to start taking better care of myself.

Finding nothing that I really wanted to watch, I turned the television off. Sighing, both bored and fatigued, I scooted farther down on the sofa. I rested my head on one of the decorative pillows and quickly drifted to sleep.

When I awakened an hour later, I was greeted by the familiar smile that had only moments ago consumed my dreams.

"*Hej*," Sergei said, his soft-spoken Russian accent giving the Swedish greeting an interesting sound.

"*Hej*," I said back, actually allowing myself to be pleased to see him. I mentally reasoned that it was mostly out of gratitude for the kindness he'd shown to me through my illness. I sat up and pushed a hand back through my hair, trying to make it look a little better. Then I figured since he had already seen it in even worse condition, it really didn't matter much.

Sergei stood and moved his chair closer. "How are you feeling?" His sincere gaze held mine against my will.

"I'm better today." I tried to pull my eyes away from his but wasn't able to this time.

"I am glad. I was very worried about you."

What is it about this man that keeps tugging at a part of me I don't want touched, that I don't want any man to get near? I wondered. And why was the wall surrounding my heart beginning to weaken despite my best efforts? Pondering these questions, I suddenly felt the need to thank him for his kindness.

"I appreciate all you've done. Thank you."

"I am glad that I could be here," he said. The expression on his face seemed to silently add, *I wouldn't want to be anywhere else.*

I smiled back timidly and asked, "How was your trip?"

"It was good," he answered, leaning forward and resting his elbows on his thighs. "It is always good to see my family."

"You went back to Russia?" I was genuinely interested.

He smiled and nodded. "The only way I get see them is if I go there. I do not think my parents or my sister and her husband will ever move away." His smile faded slightly. "I do not think they will ever understand my need to move away, either." He paused and smiled again. "Every time I talk to my mother, the first thing she says to me is, '*Seriozha*, you should move back home. You need to be with family.' And my sister follows up with '*Serioque*, come home.'"

"*Seriozha*? *Serioque*?" I questioned. "Are those nick

51

names?"

His eyes met mine. "They are names used by people I am close to."

Seriozha. Serioque. I ignored the slight skip of my heart as I repeated each name in my mind and pulled my thoughts back to what we had been discussing. "I take it you don't like Russia," I said, glancing down at his clasped hands. I thought they were beautiful hands, strong looking but beautiful.

"I love Russia," he said, his expression thoughtful. "I will always love Russia. But I love freedom more."

I nodded, understanding and needing no other explanation. "Grandma said you've lived in Sweden for about a year now."

"*Da.* This is true." He smiled. "It was right after I moved here that I met Felicity and Karl."

I grinned. "They grow on you rather quickly, don't they?"

"Ah, this is true as well," he said with a grin of his own. "They are wonderful people." He paused, adding, "And they love you very much."

Not knowing what to say, I looked away, again wondering just how much my grandparents had shared with him. If they did tell him about my past, I wondered what he must think of me. Did he think I was weak? Or just plain stupid, or even beneath him?

Why did I even care now?

If I didn't know any better, I would swear that my grandparents had been praying about me behind my back, because things that didn't matter before suddenly seemed to now.

I also wondered if Sergei could read my thoughts, because in that next instant, he leaned forward, covered my hand with his large, warm one and said, "I am sorry for what you have gone through, Heaven. No woman deserves to be treated the way you have been. No one deserves the sorrow you have experienced in your life."

No, I won't do this now, especially in front of him! Be strong. Be strong . . .

I blinked furiously against the sudden burning behind my eyes, but a couple of tears managed to escape anyway. "Thank you," I finally said, trying to smile.

When he reached out and wiped my tears with his gentle hand, the emotions I had been holding back for weeks came to the surface, and I couldn't seem to stop them. One by one, the memories came, each one marked by both emotional and physical pain.

The beatings.

The belittling.

The neglect.

The abandonment.

The feeling of aloneness.

Sensing my pain and my need for release, Sergei moved to the edge of the sofa, gently pulled me into the haven of his arms, and let me cry. I pressed my face against his warm chest and cried more at that moment than I had in my entire life. I think the tears that came at that moment *were* for my whole life, for every painful thing I had ever gone through.

I tried to get a hold of my emotions, but I couldn't. His strong arms tightened around me and I burrowed deeper in his embrace, soaking in the comfort he gave. It was like giving water to someone dying of thirst. I had been emotionally depleted for far too long.

Feeling like an idiot for letting my emotions get the best of me, I took a deep breath and slowly drew back. "I'm sorry," I said, looking at the tear-stained spot on his shirt.

"Look at me, Heaven" he said, taking my face between his hands. When I raised my eyes, I saw the tears in his, and it surprised me.

"You have nothing to be sorry for." He brushed another tear away with his thumb but kept my face in his hands. "But you need to learn to trust again." Releasing my face, he took my hands in his. "There are evil people in the world, but there are also good ones."

I closed my eyes briefly and sighed. "I know." I looked at him intently. "But so much has happened. Trusting again will be very hard for me."

Lifting a warm hand again to my face, he said simply, "Then start with me."

Warmed by his compassion, I smiled. I had never known anyone like him before, except for the Copeland family and my grandparents, but this was different.

He made me *feel* different.

I was still afraid, but seeing the expectant look in his eyes, I nodded. "I'll try."

Sergei remained silent for a moment, his eyes studying my face. When his brow furrowed slightly, I knew he was momentarily deep in thought. I ached to know what he was thinking at that moment but felt too shy to ask. I wanted so badly to lift my hand and gently smooth his brow.

Suddenly smiling at me, he wiped at my tears once more. "Can I do anything for you?"

"No, but I would like to talk some more, unless you need to leave." I silently hoped he didn't.

"Nothing is more important than being here with you."

I smiled shyly and moved my legs off the sofa to make room for him to sit, but as soon as he sat down, he lifted my legs and placed them across his lap, wanting me to still be comfortable.

And I *was* comfortable, even sitting with him this way. Strangely, it felt natural.

We talked for a long while. I shared more about myself

and my life before moving to Stockholm, expounding on the things he already knew. I shared details about my mother, and Ross. Having released my emotions earlier, it wasn't as painful talking about those things as I thought it would be.

Sergei then told me about his parents, his sister, Martina, and her husband, Alexander. He shared with me stories of his childhood and growing up with very little. He also told me about his hockey career and the knee injury that ended it. He said he was sorry about the injury, but not about retiring. It had been time.

"Isn't hockey pretty dangerous?" I asked.

"It can be, especially if tempers are lost."

"It seems like that happens frequently. Was it ever dangerous for you?"

"Hmmm, let me see." He smiled slightly. "I remember scoring the winning goal in a game and the goalie of the opposing team got angry. After we took off our head gear he approached me, lost his temper and hit me."

"No way! What did you do?"

He grinned. "I lost my temper and hit him back, of course." When I laughed, he added, "He was not a happy loser."

"Of course not," I said, grinning at his smug expression.

During a lull in the conversation, Grandma entered, carrying a tray with two glasses of juice and some of her luscious pastries. Her eyebrows raised slightly at the sight of my legs across Sergei's lap, but I was too famished to care at that moment. Having eaten only broth and crackers for the past couple of days, the fluffy pastries looked wonderful.

"*Tack*," Sergei said, taking the tray from her and placing it on the coffee table.

"*Varsagod*," Grandma said in return and I found myself grateful for the bit of Swedish I had learned. Of course, thank you and you're welcome were basic, but truthfully, I understood a lot more than I could speak.

After she left us, we ate and talked some more. I wasn't surprised to learn that Sergei was thirty-four, but with his ruggedly handsome features and perfect build, he looked younger. There was no need to tell him my age because my grandmother told him when she inquired about the housekeeping job for me. True, I was an adult, but compared to Sergei, in some ways I felt like a child. Still, I was twenty-one and had seen and experienced much. Naivety wasn't something I could completely claim.

"Did you enjoy your time in America?" I asked, taking a bite of a frosted cake.

"I did," he answered. "It is a very beautiful country."

I nodded. "What did you do while you were there?"

"Well, most of the time, I visited historical sites across the country and learned as much as I could. My favorite states were Massachusetts, Pennsylvania, and of course, Utah because of the Church." He paused and smiled. "I have always been fascinated with America's history."

"America does have an amazing heritage." I smiled, suddenly feeling a little melancholy. "I miss a lot of people there."

"You miss the family that took you in," Sergei stated, having read my feelings in my expression. When I nodded, he said, "Maybe you can go back to see them sometime."

I blinked the sudden tears back and shook my head. In my heart I knew that wasn't possible. "Not as long as Ross is still around."

Sergei gave me an understanding nod and took one of my hands in his again, caressing the back of it with his thumb.

"One day," he said, looking into my eyes, "you will feel safe again." He turned his body slightly and touched my face. "I want to help you feel safe again." He pushed the hair back from my face and pressed his hand against my cheek once more. "Will you let me try?"

I looked away, not knowing what to say or how to answer. This man had burrowed his way into my heart without even trying, and I didn't know what to make of it.

When I said nothing, he said with fervor, "I will never hurt you, Heaven."

Feeling warmth slowly surround me, I knew it was time

to stop fighting and at least try to start trusting again. I lifted my hand and placed it over the one he held to my face. Then, looking into his soulful eyes I said, "I know you won't." And somewhere deep inside me, I really *did* know.

As he continued to look at me, I felt an overwhelming need to apologize to him. "Sergei, I have been so distant to you, yet you never stopped being kind to me. I'm so sorry for . . ."

He pressed a gentle finger to my lips. "There is nothing to be sorry for. Truly, I understand." He ran the same finger down my cheek and smiled.

I smiled back, feeling my cheeks warm and looked shyly away.

Sergei stayed and talked with me through the afternoon. At one point he looked at his watch and whistled, surprised at the time. So was I. He grinned."Well, since I am here and it is dinner time, I would like to go out and get dinner for us and your grandparents. Would that be all right?"

I grinned. "You mean you aren't tired of listening to me yet?"

He smoldering gaze caused warmth to spread through me. Never in my life had I been so affected by a look.

"I could never be tired of talking with you, Heaven." He squeezed my hand gently. "I could never tire of being with you period."

I glanced down again, not knowing what to say. After a moment, I looked up and met his steady gaze again. "The feeling is mutual." He lifted my hand to his lips and pressed a kiss there, and my heart threatened to thump right through my chest.

As Sergei left to go and get the food, I leaned back against the pillows and closed my eyes and sighed over these unexpected events.

Then I slowly smiled.

My heart told me there would be no turning back now.

And I felt okay with that.

Eight

On the following Monday I was completely well and returned to work. Only things were not the same now. I was not the same. I was beginning to feel like my old self again, even better than my old self. And it was mainly because of Sergei. Somehow, he'd found the part of me that had been lost.

Dusting a brass-framed picture on a wall in the library, I smiled as memories of the time we'd spent together washed over me.

Sergei had come to see me every day during the past week. As I gained my strength back, we began going out for short walks around Old Town. A couple of times we had lunch or dinner at one of the sidewalk restaurants and at night, we sat and talked until late.

On Sunday he picked me up and we attended church together. It felt both strange and wonderful to have him by my side in sacrament meeting and Sunday school, and I didn't feel so alone. Very fluent in Swedish, he introduced me to some of the members I hadn't met the previous week. He stayed close to me, keeping my hand possessively in his every moment. If it had have been anyone else, this action would've scared me, but not with Sergei. Nothing about him frightened me.

That evening we had an enjoyable dinner with my grandparents, and thankfully, they didn't ask any uncomfortable questions about us or make any insinuations. Then we went back to Sergei's house, had some Russian apple and walnut strudel he'd made the day before, and talked some more.

We ended the night watching a movie in the theater room. I had felt an indescribable comfort nestled in his arms. I felt safe and cared for. The latter had been needed more than I realized. At the movie's end, Sergei gently awakened me because I had fallen asleep, and took me home.

I couldn't believe how much I enjoyed just being with him. I loved the feel of my hand nestled in his large one. I loved the way he looked at me when I talked, giving me his full attention, the way he studied my expressions. I loved looking at him. Oh, how I loved that! Sometimes we just sat and silently stared at one another. During those times I felt more beautiful than I ever had in my life.

As I continued dusting the library, I contemplated our relationship. I could say we were good friends, but we were more than that. We hadn't really labeled what we were to one another because we couldn't at the moment, but I knew how Sergei felt without him saying the words. It was in his every gaze, his every action.

So far, we had only shared embraces and gentle caresses. He smelled so good and his arms were so warm and safe, I truly relished the embraces. I was beginning to crave them, and that made me feel vulnerable at times. Still, Sergei never pushed his affections on me. He knew he needed to be patient with me, and he had been. In the short amount of time I had known him, I had grown to trust him more than I thought I could ever trust anyone. I wondered how he had become so important to me and how I had come to feel so close to him.

What happened to my adamant decision to stay away from men?

How had Sergei ingrained himself in my heart so? How had he been able to reach inside me, take my fears and throw them away?

Is it because he is so much older than me? I questioned silently. *Is it the age difference that makes me feel so safe with him?*

After pondering this for another moment, I decided it wasn't that. I concluded that the reason he made me feel this way was because of the kind of man he is. There are no pretenses about him, and his heart was completely open to me. So open that all I needed to do was say the word or give him a signal and he would move forward. But I didn't know if I was ready for that yet.

I was dusting the last bookshelf when Sergei entered. Just the sight of him made my heart skip a beat, and the warmth of his endearing smile, the feel of his longing gaze, seem to light up my whole world. He had no idea how much his mere presence affected me.

"Hi," I said as he approached me.

"Hello." He smiled and took my hand in his. "Do you need to be anywhere after you are done today?"

"Not really. Why?"

"Well, I thought it would be nice to have a picnic dinner out on the back lawn. Will you join me?"

I squeezed his hand and smiled. "I'd love to."

He lifted my hand and kissed it. The feel of his soft lips again caused warmth to spread through me. He stood looking down at me a moment longer and I could see the emotion in his eyes.

Whether I was ready or not, something was about to change between us. Everything in me could sense it. His warm eyes held mine captive a moment longer before he left me to finish. I still felt his presence long after he had gone. I liked that

Nine

I called Grandma and told her I would be home late, which greatly pleased her. To Grandma, every moment I was away meant more time for me to be with Sergei, and that made her extremely happy. Just like Sergei, her heart was open to me, and I knew her hopes for me.

After I hung up, I went to the kitchen and found Sergei closing a picnic basket. As he turned to me and smiled, I felt butterflies inside. Standing there staring at me with unmasked adoration, Sergei was irresistible, and I felt myself falling even more. At that very moment my heart became completely lost to him. I smiled back, emotion welling up inside me.

He took my hand and led me through the French patio

doors. After walking out a ways, we stopped at a spot near the gazebo and spread a blanket out on the grass. We sat side by side as the afternoon sun warmed us. I looked up and watched a flock of seagulls fly overhead, their energetic calls adding a peacefulness to the moment. The evening sky was still a brilliant blue and because of the time of year, darkness didn't settle on the country until midnight. Falling asleep had been a little weird for me at first, but I was finally used to it.

Since we had spent so much time the week before talking of deeper things and getting to know one another, Sergei and I decided to spend this time talking about trivial things, things that wouldn't matter to anyone but us. Things like our favorite books, our favorite movies, favorite foods, favorite things to do. We talked about our likes and dislikes. We laughed as we compared our similar tastes in comedies, our dislikes of certain vegetables, and our mutual love for rainy days and sloshing through puddles on the sidewalk after a heavy downpour.

Sergei also shared with me his hopes of having his family join the Church one day. He told me how hard it was for him sometimes to not be able to share that part of his life with them, and he knew I understood.

After we had finished eating and the conversation had comfortably wound down, Sergei leaned back on his elbows, stretched out his long legs, and crossed his ankles, his eyes resting on my face. I met his steady gaze, not able to pull mine away.

As I took in the emotions I saw in his eyes, something stirred inside me. It was as if all the emotional energy in the world suddenly zeroed in on the two of us, producing a magnetic pull that I couldn't fight anymore.

I continued to stare into his eyes and I knew he felt it too. As if our coming together was inevitable, he raised up slightly, lifted a hand to my face, and let his thumb softly caress the corner of my mouth, moving it slowly over my lips. My heart was pounding so hard, I almost felt like I couldn't breathe. I felt myself slowly moving down to him. When my mouth was an inch away from his, I hesitated as a subtle fear quickly entered me.

Sensing this, Sergei whispered softly, "You own my heart, *dushenka*, and I will never hurt you."

The warmth of his breath on my face combined with the sound of his deep voice whispering the tender Russian term of endearment brought about a heated rush of emotion in me. My breath quickened as he rose a little more and pressed his mouth to mine. And in that moment, everything inside me suddenly cried out for him, the desperate yearning to be loved overwhelming me.

I moved my hand to his face and heard him moan softly as the kiss became warm. He drew back just enough to sit up. Then he took my face between his hands and favored me with the taste of his sweet kiss once again. His lips plied mine possessively, demandingly, yet his kiss gave to me, filling my every sense. I ached inside to be closer still.

The exhilaration I felt being with him this way was like nothing I had ever experienced before and the feelings that surged through my insides were beyond description. Nothing in this life had prepared me for the tenderness I felt, for the intoxicating wonder I was now experiencing at his hand.

I wrapped my arms around his waist and melted against him as his love continued to wash over me, washing away the hurt that had once filled me, and replacing it with an indescribable urge to trust again, to trust in him, in what we had between us.

These feelings filled me with such warmth, I parted my lips from his slightly and whispered, "I love you, *Seriozha*."

Sergei drew back a little and looked into my eyes, his own filling with tears. "I love you too, Heaven. More than I could ever express to you in words."

His mouth captured mine once more, and trembling, I hungrily accepted and returned his warm kiss. Then he lay back and pulled me down next to him. I laid my head against his chest and he wrapped his arms securely around me.

I closed my eyes and breathed deeply as the scent of the harbor filled the air and added a magical serenity to the deepening azure sky. We lay in silence, holding onto one another and relishing this moment.

I couldn't believe this was happening to me. I couldn't believe how much love I suddenly had in my heart for this man. And I marveled at the love I felt from him. When I made the decision to move to Sweden, I hadn't expected anything like this to happen. I never wanted it to. But now that it had, I felt blessed beyond words. I smiled, enjoying the feel of Sergei's hand gently caressing my hair.

After a long while, he turned me onto my back, raised up, and looked down at me. Pressing a hand to my face he smiled and said, "I never truly realized how alone I was until you came into my life."

I sighed and lightly ran my hand over the muscles of his back. "I feel the same."

Hi smile widened. "I suppose I am going to have to fire you now." When I shot him a confused look, he sobered and went on. "I do not want to just see you during the day. I want you beside me at night, wrapped in my arms. I want to feel your warmth against me when I sleep, and I want to be able to look at your beautiful face ever waking moment."

He paused, pressing his hand against my flat stomach. "I want my children to grow inside you. I want your kiss to be the last thing I taste before I fall asleep at night, and the first thing I experience when I awaken each morning." He smiled. "I cannot do those things with my housekeeper . . . but I can with my wife." He paused again, wiping the warm tears that were rolling back into my hair. "So, you see why I have to fire you?"

I swallowed hard against the emotion in my throat and nodded. "I guess I can understand that," I finally said.

He looked at me intently. "Will you be my wife?"

I nodded again, too overcome to speak.

Sergei leaned down and lightly pressed his lips to mine. "I need you to say the word, *dushenka*," he whispered breathlessly.

I wrapped my arms around his waist, pulling him closer. "Yes," I whispered back. "Everything you want, I want, too."

He gave me a teary smile and rewarded me with the taste of his enrapturing kiss once more, and I knew my life was forever changed. Because of Sergei, I finally knew what it felt like to truly be loved, to be adored, and I also knew with everything in me, I would crave the warmth of his love forever.

Ten

It took several lengthy kisses on my grandparents' doorstep before Sergei could finally say goodbye to me, but even after saying goodbye, we couldn't bring ourselves to part, and we were soon back in each other's arms. I talked him into staying for a while, which didn't require much effort. We sat on the living room sofa holding one another and talked a little longer.

We were excited about sharing our news with my grandparents and his family. I knew how much Grandma and Grandpa wanted this for me, and until the moment Sergei and I revealed our feelings for each other, I hadn't realized how much *I* had truly wanted this. I didn't think I would ever be worthy of such a blessing.

"Do you think Karl and Felicity will approve of me marrying their granddaughter?" Sergei asked, grinning.

I laughed at his playful expression. "I think you won their approval the moment you hired me, or better yet, the moment you walked into the bakery."

"Hmmm. I wondered why they always gave me twice as many pastries as I ordered."

"You see?" I said, smiling widely. "They had it all planned. They were working on us both."

"And I will forever be grateful to them for that."

Sergei and I began to talk about the changes that would come into our lives and speculated over our future. After a while there were no more words, only the sound of my heart beating in time with his.

I leaned my head back a little and looked up at him, pressing a hand softly to his face. "You have totally changed my life, *Seriozha*. You've given me everything."

He touched my face, then caressed my lips. "You have made my life worth living." He lowered his head and whispered, "You are everything to me." Then his mouth took mine in a sublimely heated kiss that left no room for doubt.

"We will have a wonderful life," he said, releasing my lips, his voice raspy. "And I will do everything in my power to make you happy."

Burying my fingers in his soft, tousled hair, I said, "You have already made me happier than you could ever know." Then I pulled his head down and experienced the power of his kiss once more, and I knew the boundless love that burned in my heart for him would forever light my way.

After Sergei and I finally parted and I went to my room, I noticed a brown envelope on the foot of the bed. It was from Shirley. Smiling with anticipation, I quickly changed into my pajamas, said my prayers, and sat on the bed. I excitedly opened the envelope to find another envelope inside with a note attached written in Shirley's handwriting.

Heaven,

Your friend from the apartment complex dropped by some paper you left behind. She said her name was Gwen. I told her I would forward them to you.

Love,

Shirley

I stared at the sealed envelope for a moment. I didn't know anyone by that name, and though I didn't know every tenant in the complex, deep inside I felt sure there was no

Gwen living there.

My heart lurched in a way it hadn't since leaving Tennessee. Taking a deep breath, I opened the envelope and pulled out a set of papers. Except for the top sheet, they were all blank. Ross' handwriting stood out from the page. I closed my eyes and moaned harshly. He had probably paid the person to drop the letter off at John and Shirley's. Either that, or he used his looks and what little charms he still possessed to persuade some unsuspecting bimbo to impersonate this fictitious person. I wouldn't put anything past Ross. My hands were shaking as I began to read the letter.

In the letter he accused me of leaving him for no reason and said he knew there was another man. He called me ungrateful and worthless among other things. I wiped the tears streaking my face as I read the last part of the letter.

We were so good together, Heaven, but you threw it all away. I gave you everything and tried to be the best man I could be for you, but nothing was ever enough. I was never good enough. Why couldn't you see that we belonged together? We belong together still.

You are mine, Heaven. I own you and always will. You hurt me bad, honey, and one day you are going to pay for leaving me. It's only a matter of time before you come back. And when you do, I will be waiting.

I squeezed my eyes shut and moaned again. *This man is insane!*

Still trembling, I ripped up the letter and tossed the pieces into the wastepaper basket by the table. I dried my tears and took a deep breath to calm myself.

I'm here and he's there. I'm safe and everything will be okay. I held my hands out in front of me and tried to stop them from shaking, telling myself to get a grip.

I won't let him do this to me. I'm moving on.

I finally slipped into bed and turned out the light. Closing my eyes, Ross' face appeared before me and his voice rang in my ears. I turned the lamp back on and his face faded.

I said a silent prayer that everything would indeed be all right. And I left the light on.

Eleven

Hearing myself moan loudly I jerked awake. Beads of sweat covered my forehead and my pillow was damp. I turned and looked at the clock.

It was only three-thirty in the morning.

And I was trembling.

The reoccurring nightmare that had stopped a couple of weeks before was now back. I wiped a hand across my forehead and sat up. My first thought was one of gratitude—gratitude for the knowledge that it had only been a dream. My second was of Sergei.

Sergei, the angel who loved me.

Sergei, the beautiful, amazing man who pledged his heart and soul to me, yet had no idea of how grievous the baggage coming with me really was.

Would it always be this way? Would my past be continually lurking, waiting to come between us? Could I honestly make him happy?

Pulling my knees up, I closed my eyes and rested my head against them. Then the tears came. I didn't know if I could go through with this. I loved Sergei with every fiber of my being, but I didn't know if I could bind him to me knowing I could go off the deep end at any minute. He deserved better than that.

Will I have any peace, Father?

My internal question was met with silence.

I lay back down and pulled the covers over me, my damp skin beginning to chill. I again told myself I could not let Ross steal my happiness.

If only I would listen to myself.

If only I could believe it.

Two hours later I was still awake.

I needed Sergei.

It was early and I knew I would most likely be waking him, but I called him anyway. As soon as I heard his sleep-filled voice, the tears came.

"It's me," I managed to say. "I'm sorry to call you so early."

"It is all right, angel. What is wrong?"

The concern in his voice brought my emotions completely to the surface again. "I need you." My voice broke.

"I am on my way."

I met Sergei at the door. Once inside, he immediately pulled me into his arms and I clung to him.

"I am here," he soothed. "I am here, baby."

We went up to my room. He sat on the bed and held me on his lap, rocking me back and forth. I continued to cling to him, grateful to have his arms around me. As long as I was sheltered in his embrace, the fears went away.

"Talk to me, *dushenka*," he said after a long while. "What is troubling you?"

"Nothing," I said against his shoulder. I couldn't bring myself to tell him about the dream or the letter. "I just needed you. I needed to have you hold me, to hear you say you love me, and that everything will be okay."

Sergei pulled back a little and looked into my eyes. I could see him trying to read in them what I didn't say, what I couldn't say. I knew he didn't understand. How could he? How could I explain to him that there was still a part of me he didn't know, a part of me that was still frightened to the core of my past?

He must have seen something there because his eyes quickly misted. He pressed a gentle hand to my face. "I love you, Heaven, more than anything else in the world" He kissed my lips. "Everything will be all right," he whispered.

"Promise me," I pleaded.

He pulled me tightly against him. "I promise, baby." He kissed me again and murmured, "I promise."

Tennessee

Ross leaned back in the leather recliner and closed his eyes, soaking in the darkness of the living room, his right hand holding a glass of vodka, and contemplated his next move. He had temporarily lost something he was determined to get back.

If Heaven thought she could just walk away from him, she had better think again. He had invested too much time and emotion in her and he wasn't about to let it all go to waste. No matter what she thought, she was his, and she would always be.

He lifted the glass to his lips and took a healthy swallow, grimacing slightly as the burning liquid rolled down his throat and heated his already warm insides. It seemed he was drinking more these days, and of course, it was Heaven's fault. Drinking was the only way he could sooth his emotions. There were plenty of women who were willing to ease his loneliness, and he had been with a few, but the hour or two spent in their willing arms meant nothing to him. The ease of which they succumbed to him disgusted him, causing thoughts of violence to surged through him when he was with them, yet he stayed his hand. Well, all but once, but he'd managed to keep the girl quiet so far. He wasn't about to risk ruining everything over mindless bimbos who would most likely send the law after him for a little roughness. No, he couldn't let that happen. Nothing would stand in the way of him getting his property back.

Nobody leaves me! he mentally shouted. *Nobody!*

Twelve

One month later

The tears glistening on Sergei's face matched my own as the sealer pronounced us married for eternity. The moment I heard those words was the happiest of my life, because I knew I was now bound to the man I loved more than life. My grandfather had been right. God did know what was best for me. He had blessed me with what had been best for me, and that was Sergei's love.

Shirley and John had flown in a couple of days before and I was happy beyond words to have them there to share this special time in my life with. They both loved Sergei from the moment they met him and he felt the same about them.

As Shirley smiled tearfully at me from across the sealing room, I couldn't help remembering the conversation she and I had the night they arrived. She told me how much she and John had prayed that I would find someone who would love me and take care of me. I told her their prayers had joined my grandparents', and God had been listening.

As we accepted hugs from our guests at the conclusion of the ceremony, my own smile faded slightly as I thought back on certain parts of my conversation with Shirley.

"That man is a blessing, Heaven. And I only have to look in his eyes to see how much he loves you. When you two are together, it's as if no one else exists." Then she added mischievously, "Of course, with a striking figure of a man like that, who would blame you? I mean, I might be old and married, but I know handsome when I see it, and let me tell you, that man probably sends a lot of female temperatures rising."

I laughed and shook my head. Leave it to Shirley to say exactly what was on her mind. "I'm sure you're right, but the rest of the female population will just have to either find a way to cool down or suffer heat stroke because he's all mine."

Shirley chuckled. "I couldn't have said it better myself, honey."

I smiled. "Oh Shirley, he's the most amazing man I've ever known, and he's totally changed my life." I sighed. "I can't tell you how good it feels to trust again. He makes me feel so safe, and I know he will never hurt me. I mean, we aren't even married yet and he puts my needs before

82

his own. He makes me feel so secure."

Shirley smiled at me tearfully. "That is what real love is all about. That's the way things should be."

We talked for a while longer and she filled me in on what was going on in their busy lives. At one point during the conversation, Shirley became unusually quiet, and I could see a subtle look of worry in her expression. I asked her if anything was wrong. She said that she hated to bring up a bad subject during such a happy occasion, but she needed to tell me something.

"What is it?" I asked, suddenly worried.

She placed her hand over mine and patted it lightly. "Well, I don't want to worry you, but . . . the other day Sue was doing some shopping in the store you worked in . . . and Ross was there. She said he was asking questions about you."

The statement instantly brought back the fear I felt when I received the letter from Ross. I lightly pressed a hand to my heart, feeling it pound a little harder. The last thing I wanted or needed was Ross asking around about me. "What was he asking?" My voice sounded calmer than I felt.

"Well, he wanted to know if anyone had heard from you."

"Did she say he found out anything?" I asked, hoping Sue's eavesdropping skills were still in place. Having been raised with the girl, many things that should have been secret, I found out from Sue.

"The girl he questioned suggested that . . .maybe you had gone to live with your grandparents . . . and that's as far as the conversation went." When I squeezed my eyes shut and groaned, Shirley hurried on quickly. "He doesn't know for sure, Heaven. When he came to our house

after you left asking us where you had gone, we told him you went to stay with some friends for a while in North Carolina. We tried to make the story sound convincing by telling him not to try and find you there." Shirley chuckled harshly. "Oh, he tried to convince us of how much he loved you by turning on the waterworks and telling us he was sorry for the way he treated you. He even said he was getting some counseling, but we didn't buy his act one bit. And after the way he underhandedly got us to send you that letter, I know he hasn't changed, and he never will."

I pressed my head in my hands as the familiar fear again entered my heart. "He's going to come after me, isn't he?" I knew the answer to my question before I even voiced it, because I knew Ross. I knew him better than anyone. If he really wanted to find me, he definitely had the means to do it.

"I doubt he will come this far looking for you," Shirley said, trying to ease my fear. "Besides, you are getting married the day after tomorrow. And even if he did manage to find you, which I'm sure he won't, it wouldn't matter. Sergei loves you and he will keep you safe." She squeezed my hand. "Don't worry, Heaven. Everything will be all right."

Deciding to take her advice, I took a deep breath and did my best to put it out of my mind. I didn't want thoughts of Ross to mar our wedding day, so I focused my thoughts on Sergei instead. I had to, because he knew me so well, he would have known something was wrong.

Well, at least I made it through the ceremony without a single thought of Ross. That was something.

Afterward, we had a light wedding luncheon at Sergei's, which was now *my* home as well. My grandparents catered the food as a wedding present for us. They hadn't been able to attend the ceremony, but I never saw two happier people, except for me any my new husband, of course.

Many ward members and a few of Sergei's friends attended the luncheon. There were even a few of my grandparents' friends there. I didn't know them, but I guess it didn't matter. I was Karl and Felicity's granddaughter, and that was all that mattered to them.

John and Shirley decided to stay in Sweden a few extra days, so we left an extra key with them and told them to enjoy the house. They assured us they would.

We were disappointed that Sergei's family hadn't come for the reception, but they promised him they would come for a visit soon. Sergei said he hoped they really would, but he wouldn't hold his breath. I assured him that there was always hope.

Later on that afternoon, we boarded a plane to Amsterdam for our honeymoon. Neither of us had ever been there before, but we were told how beautiful the city was and we were excited about going. Sergei told me Amsterdam was only one of the many places he wanted to take me. I looked forward to traveling with him. It wouldn't matter to me where we went as long as we were together.

Sergei kept my hand in his, his gaze fixed on mine as the plane left the runway. He leaned over slightly and kissed me tenderly.

"I love you, Mrs. Petrenko," he whispered.

I smiled dreamily, loving the sound of my new name. "And I love you." His mouth curved up in a returning smile and I couldn't resist kissing him again.

He put his arm around me and I rested my head against his shoulder, relishing the feelings of love and security that now washed over me. In his embrace I felt like nothing could touch me, and no harm could ever come to me. Sighing, I drifted to sleep with the feel of his soft lips against my forehead, and memories of our wedding filling my thoughts.

After a while and against my will, a different face began to swim before me, one that frightened me beyond words. It was Ross' face. I felt one of his hands tugging at my hair, the other, tugging at my clothes. I heard his voice repeating what he'd said to me the last night I saw him in Knoxville.

"*I will finally have what's mine.*"

I heard myself gasp as I awakened to the hum of the

airplane engines as we made our descent into Amsterdam.

"Are you all right?" Sergei's soothing voice asked, holding me close.

I nodded, not able to speak at the moment. I almost felt like I was going to be sick. I swallowed back the feeling, but the dream had seemed so real, I felt afraid again.

"What is it?" Sergei asked, concern filling his voice.

I shook my head and tried to smile. "It's nothing, just a bad dream." I leaned over and kissed him. "I'll be fine."

"Are you sure?" he asked, and I could tell he wasn't totally convinced.

I smiled. "I'm sure."

As we rode in the taxi to our hotel, I did my best to push my fears aside and instead concentrated on the amazing scenery. There were canals running through Amsterdam in every direction, and the massive stone buildings draped in bright shades of cloth were beautiful. Never in my life had I seen anything like it. It had to be the most colorful city I had ever been in, even more so than Stockholm.

I turned to Sergei and found him gazing at me instead of the scenery. The loving look in his eyes was tinged with worry. I squeezed his hand, trying to assure him that all was well. I only wished I could assure myself.

Later, I stood in front of the bedroom window of our suite wearing a white silk and lace chemise I bought for this night. My eyes took in the view of the enormous city, but my mind focused on none of it. Rubbing my arms against a sudden chill, I closed my burning eyes, willing the tears to stay away, but they came anyway. I quickly dried them, not wanting to worry Sergei.

I couldn't believe this was happening. This was my wedding day! There shouldn't have been tears of sadness, only tears of joy. I couldn't understand why I couldn't control my emotions. And hard as I tried, I couldn't seem to stop my fears from intruding upon what was supposed to be our time, mine and Sergei's.

My hands involuntarily formed fists as an internal battle of emotions waged within me. My fear of Ross seemed to mingle with my longing for my husband, and I didn't know how to separate the two. I couldn't.

When Sergei entered the bedroom, I tensed slightly despite my best efforts. I managed to smile. He smiled back, and I read the desire in his warm brown eyes. As he walked toward me, I felt my smile fade slightly. He gazed down at me and gently took my shoulders in his hands. Feeling my eyes begin to burn again, I looked down.

"What is it, angel?" he asked softly. He rubbed my arms.

"You are trembling." He lifted my chin, urging me to look at him. "Please tell me what is wrong."

Sergei's desperate plea drew my emotions to the surface, and before I knew it, my face was pressed against his warm chest as my tears wet his shirt. He lifted me in his arms and carried me over to the bed. He sat down and held me on his lap. He kept his arms wrapped around me and continued to let me cry.

I figured by now he was definitely wondering what he had gotten himself into. The woman he married was an emotional wreck, and he had no idea why. I felt sorry for him.

After I was finally able to get a hold of my emotions, I pulled back slightly and took in his worried expression. "I'm so sorry," I finally said.

Sergei lifted a gentle hand to my face and dried my tears. "Please, Heaven," he pleaded again. "It hurts me to see your tears. Tell me what is wrong."

Gathering my courage, I looked into his eyes and tearfully told him about my conversation with Shirley. I didn't tell him about the letter, but I shared with him my fears of Ross coming to find me.

He sat silently listening to me until I had finished. Then taking my face in his hands, he said, "Shirley told me everything last night."

I stared at him, my surprise evident. "Everything?" I

asked, wondering if that included the letter.

Seeming to understand the tone of my question, he said, "Yes, everything."

"Then you know why I am worried."

Sergei sighed. "Do not be worried, my love. You are my wife now. We are bound to each other, and I will never let anyone hurt you. Please trust me." He closed his eyes and pressed his forehead to mine. "Please trust me, baby," he whispered again.

I closed my eyes and exhaled softly, a heady longing suddenly filling me at the feel of his warm breath on my face.

"Please trust me, angel," he whispered once more before his warm mouth took mine.

His words were now in Russian, but my heart understood them, and before I knew it, our bodies and our souls were suddenly intertwined as he made love to me, erasing all fear, all pain, and all doubt from my mind and my heart. All that existed then, all that I was aware of, was his love. And experiencing that love, truly experiencing the magnitude of it, was the most wondrous and glorious thing I had ever known.

Every kiss, every gentle touch, every softly spoken word whispered from his lips against mine, pulled me further into safety, further into the safe harbor that was his love. That wondrously fulfilling safety was now my home, and it was there that I knew I would always stay.

Thirteen

The next morning I awakened to the warmth of Sergei's muscular arms around me. I quietly gazed at his face as he lay sleeping and couldn't resist touching the shadow of stubble on his cheek. My mind and heart marveled anew that this man was now my husband. I couldn't help wondering what I had done to deserve such a blessing. I continued to caress his face, then softly trailed a finger across his lips.

He slowly opened his eyes and smiled at me, causing me to melt inside. Somehow I knew he would always have that effect on me.

"Good morning," he said, his voice raspy.

I moved forward and pressed a soft kiss to his lips. "Good morning."

"Mmmm" he growled as he held me closer. "I am very glad that you decided to give up your housekeeping position and marry me instead."

I smiled and pressed my face in the hollow of his neck, breathing in the scent that was his. "I am too. I like the added benefits of this job."

"Really? Added benefits? What added benefits?" Sergei asked, teasing.

"This, for one," I said, kissing him warmly, igniting the passion between us once more.

A long while later he said, "I appreciate those benefits as well."

Sergei and I spent half the day touring Dam Square, the main tourist area of Amsterdam. I kept a hold of his hand as we wove back and forth, making our way through the large crowds.

I took pictures of the entire square, including numerous ones of the Royal Palace to add to my collection of photos of Stockholm's Royal Palace. Both buildings were indescribable.

We did some shopping for souvenirs. We even bought a couple of pairs of wooden clogs. I didn't know how often I would wear mine, but they were pretty to look at.

We enjoyed a delicious brunch at the famed *Cafe Luxembourg*. The dining area was spacious and the atmosphere was laid back and relaxing. We dined on onion soup, Belgian shrimp croquettes, and finished up with upside down warm apple cake that Sergei declared the most delicious dessert he had ever tasted.

We spent some time in the Van Gogh Museum and I was absolutely enthralled. We were told the museum holds the largest collection of Van Gogh paintings in the world, as well as the paintings of numerous other artists. I had never really been into art, but I couldn't deny that the pieces there were incredible. Though Van Gogh's life was tragic, his works were glorious!

We went from one place to the next and I continually snapped pictures. Throughout the day Sergei would occasionally pull me into one of the small alleyways, lock me in his strong arms and steel a kiss or two. His kisses always wove such a spell of passion over me that anyone passing by usually went unnoticed. The warmth of his arms and the intoxication of his kisses made me oblivious to everything but him. And looking into his eyes as he parted his lips from mine, I could tell that I had the same effect on him.

It truly felt wonderful to be in love.

That evening after dinner, we went to a jazz concert, and spent a lot of time out on the dance floor. Sergei was a terrific dancer, and the envious stares of the women around us made me marvel anew that I was blessed with this amazing man as my husband.

By the middle of the evening we returned to our intimate table in the corner and spent the rest of it completely wrapped up in each other, sharing warm conversation, loving gazes, and tender kisses. And though we were having an enjoyable time, we looked forward with anticipation to being alone again.

Our time in Amsterdam was amazing and memorable. And I would cherish it always, just as I would every single moment I was able to be with Sergei.

Fourteen

Never in my life had I ever dreamed I could be so happy, and never had I felt so loved. Sergei made every moment we spent together count and we never tired of being together.

Our days were filled with warm conversation, fun, laughter, and loving, always loving. Sergei was very spontaneous. We would be sitting quietly reading in the library one moment, then he was chasing me through the house, trying to tickle me the next.

I could be in the kitchen cooking dinner and he'd put on some music and suddenly pull me into his arms to dance. Or

I'd be out on the back patio where he was lounging and *accidentally* squirt him with the hose while watering the flowers. He would chase me around the house. When he caught me, he would laugh, pick me up and sling me over his shoulder, then carry me upstairs and toss me onto our bed. And there we would stay.

Not a day passed that he didn't make me laugh or smile, and I tried to do the same for him. He had become my whole life and what I felt when I was with him could not be put into words. He made me whole. He gave my life meaning, and I knew I would never be able to survive without his love. Because he had become a part of me. His essence filled me, sustained me. And I knew it always would. I was truly happy. Sergei was my happiness.

I was paralyzed with fear as Ross cornered me in the dimly lit room. I tried to escape his grip, but his fingers were like a steel vice closing around my wrists.

"Please, Ross," I begged. "Please let me go."

Ross smiled and yanked me forward, kissing me forcefully. I tried to pull away, but he was too strong. Repulsed more by the second, I bit his lip. He yelled and pulled back, and I could see the blood on his mouth, taste it on my own lips.

"You're going to pay for that," he said, coldly. "You're going to pay, then I am going to have what's mine."

He released one of my arms and hit me. I again tried to pull away, but he was too strong.

"Sergei!" I yelled. "Sergei, help me!"

Ross laughed. "Call him all you want. He can't hear you."

Suddenly Ross moved aside and pointed to the corner. My eyes moved to the object lying there and I froze. "Nooo!" I screamed as my gaze fell on Sergei's lifeless body, blood covering his chest. "No! No! No!"

"It is all right," Sergei's voice softly said as I jerked awake. "It is all right." He pulled me into his arms and I clung to him, not able to hold back the sobs. "Shhh," he whispered against my brow. "Everything is all right. It was just a bad dream."

To me it had been completely real. "Please don't let him find us!" I said with a hiccup. My whole body was shaking. "Don't let him find us! He'll try to kill you!"

Sergei held on to me tightly and I buried my face against his chest. "I promise, baby, no one will hurt you, or me."

"Oh, *Serioque*, I would die if anything happened to you," I sobbed and hiccuped again. "I would just die."

"Shhh," he whispered, pressing his mouth to mine. "We will be fine. You are mine, and no one will ever hurt you." He scattered kisses over my face and neck and continued to whisper passionately, You are mine, only mine." Pressing his lips against my ear, he began to softly croon in Russian. Then his mouth quickly took mine again.

The power of Sergei's kiss slowly calmed my fears, replacing them with an aching need for him. I felt his tears fall onto my face as he took my pain into himself. He continued to whisper emotionally in his native tongue as his kisses fell like a warm rain against my skin. All at once, I became completely lost in his love, and all that existed was the fire between us. My every sense was consumed with my burning need for him. I was oblivious to everything but his touch, his kiss, and his warmth. Whenever he loved me, everything else went away, and I was safe, safe in the harbor of his love.

Long after the passion had subsided into a quiet calm, Sergei held me close. I lay awake, relishing the warmth of his embrace, knowing sleep would not come for a while.

"Talk to me, *dushenka*," Sergei said softly. "Tell me about your dream."

I shook my head, burying my face against his chest as tears again began to burn my eyes. "I can't."

He pressed his lips into my hair and sighed. "I hate him for hurting you," he growled, his voice full of pain and anger. "I know I should not, but I hate him." He released me and reached over to turn on the light. I was startled to see the hard look in his tear-filled eyes. He looked down at me, pressing a hand to my face. Then his expression softened. "He will not come here, Heaven."

"I wish I could believe that," I said.

Sergei leaned down touched his forehead to mine. "I promised you I would never let anyone hurt you. I meant that."

I touched his face. "I know."

"God is with us, *dushenka*." He raised up a little to look into my eyes. "We will be all right."

I nodded, wanting with all my heart to believe him.

"Are you going to be okay?" he asked.

I again nodded. He kissed me once more, letting his lips linger on mine for a moment before turning out the light. He wrapped me in his arms and I clung to him. "I love you so much, Sergei."

"I love you, too," he said softly and kissed my brow. "Everything will be all right."

"You promise?"

"I promise."

I closed my eyes, snuggled deeper into the warmth of his embrace, and sighed, silently praying he was right.

Fifteen

We had been married for a month when Sergei's family

came to see us. It was the first time they had ever left Russia and Sergei was amazed they actually made the trip. They told him they figured it was about time they saw some more of the world, and the best place for them to start was Sweden so they could meet their new daughter-in-law.

Sergei's mother, Oksana, was a kind woman with laughing brown eyes, graying dark hair and a heart of gold. Her whole face seemed to light up when she smiled and I loved her immediately. She frequently took my face in her hands, kissed my forehead, and said in broken English, "You sent from heaven for our Sergei." I always smiled and thanked her, telling her how blessed I was to have him.

Nikolai Petrenko, Sergei's father, was a very large man with a commanding presence who seemed very tough and no-nonsense when I first met him. But once I got to know him, I could see how much of a teddy bear he really was and I couldn't help but love him. Though Nikolai was handsome, I couldn't say Sergei really looked like his father all that much. I think his looks were a mixture of both his parents.

Sergei's sister, Martina, and her husband, Alexander Dmitriev, were both very quiet, but again, as I got to know them, they came out of their shells and we became great friends. The two also had a five year old daughter they named Oksana, after her grandmother. Throughout their visit, the little girl stuck to me like glue and I became very attached to her as well.

They brought us several wedding gifts and each one we opened took my breath away. From Oksana and Nikolai we received a beautifully crotched afghan. The delicate peach and ivory colored flowers were artfully placed and surrounded by a matching colored border. There was also a box of multi-fragrance candles and a set of crystal glasses.

From Martina and Alexander, we received a handmade lace tablecloth. They were all beautiful gifts and I knew I would treasure them always. We thanked his family for their thoughtfulness and for coming to see us.

The family only spent a week with us, but we kept them busy, showing them all the sights, and we had a wonderful and memorable time.

The day before they were scheduled to leave, Sergei and I took them all to dinner in Old Town. My grandparents went with us. They had enjoyed getting to know Sergei's family and were going to miss them almost as much as we were, having spent some time with them in the evenings when the bakery was closed.

We enjoyed a meal of grilled herring, garden vegetables, decadent breads, and a variety of desserts to die for. After the meal, we sat for a while and enjoyed comfortable conversation. My grandparents and Sergei's family sipped espresso, while we savored our hot chocolate. We talked about various things, always avoiding the topic of politics. Everyone had their own personal views but were wise enough to keep them to themselves.

After Sergei paid the check, he took my hand and we ushered the group down the various cobblestone streets, occasionally stopping in a shop or two to buy souvenirs for the family. We also stopped a couple of times to watch street performers as they worked their magic on the captivated audiences. This was one of the things I truly loved about this part of town. There was so much diversity, and there was always something interesting going on.

We stopped to listen to a small group of men and women singing Swedish folk songs. Their dated costumes were colorful, and their makeup was dramatic. Sergei moved behind me and wrapped his arms around my waist, holding me close. I sighed and smiled, wrapping my arms over his and covering his large hands with mine.

I looked around at the various faces, pausing a moment to take in the expressions of Sergei's family. Though they couldn't understand the words that were being sung, it was obvious they were still enjoying themselves. This was all still so new to them, and their expressions were continually filled with awe and excitement.

Sergei's mother, Oksana, caught my eye and smiled. I smiled back, thinking about how much I would miss her. She was soft-spoken, yet she laughed with her whole heart. It was a hearty kind of laugh that made you want to laugh, whether you were in the mood to or not. And her love for her son was obvious. I smiled as I thought back to what she'd said to me earlier that morning in the kitchen.

I had been washing dishes and she was drying. We had been working together in silence for a while when she turned to me and said in broken English, "You know, I always told *Serioque* he needs come back home and be with family. This was first thing I say each time he call." She smiled tearfully and squeezed my wet hand with her dry one. "But now I know he not need come back to Moscow, because home is here, with you." She took my face in her hands and again pressed a kiss to my forehead saying, "You are gift sent from heaven." Then she smiled.

Pulling my thoughts forward, I smiled again, grateful for my life, and grateful that I had been *sent* to Sweden.

Sergei tightened his embrace and pressed a soft kiss to my ear. "I love you, *dushenka*," he whispered.

"I love you," I said back, pressing a hand to his face. Then I closed my eyes for a moment and listened to the gentle sound of two Swedish bagpipers as they began playing the haunting tune of *Ljugaren*.

The song was the sad serenade of a mother who watched her son fall through a sheet of ice and drown on lake *Ljugaren*. I had heard the tune one other time since I'd been in Sweden, and even before learning what the song was about, I was moved by the music.

I found myself thinking about how sad the woman must have been. I couldn't begin to imagine what she must have felt, but listening to the music now, I could almost picture a fair-haired beauty standing by the lake, with eyes closed and tears streaming down her face, as she mourned the child that was now lost to her with music.

At the tune's end, I opened my eyes and joined the

crowd's applause. I watched money flying from the crowd, landing in the lined basket in front of the performers as they took another bow. Sergei, *Farmor*, and *Farfar* also tossed money in.

When the crowd began to call for an encore, the performers immediately complied. Sergei replaced his arms around me and we stood a little longer, enjoying the final song. No matter where we were or what we were doing, it always felt like heaven being in Sergei's arms. There was safety in them, and a security I had never known before. His presence gave me life, and his touch made my very soul want to to cry out, *I am alive!*

I sighed blissfully, completely content with my life, and awed by the gift of my husband's love. I had everything. Everything. Oh, if everyone could be as happy as I!

Contemplating the serenity I felt, I smiled and again let my eyes slowly move around the crowd when my breath caught. I briefly thought I saw something that literally made my heart stop for a second. I gasped softly and closed my eyes, doing my best to convinced myself it had only been my imagination.

"What is it?" Sergei asked, concern filling his voice.

I opened my eyes, furiously scanning the crowd, but seeing nothing.

Sergei turned me to face him. "What is it?" he asked

again. As he took in my expression, lines of worry appeared around his eyes.

I gripped his arms tightly. "I thought I saw Ross" I whispered, not wanting to alarm the others.

Sergei, sensing this, said nothing, but I watched his eyes quickly scan the crowd. Turning me back in his arms, he pressed me back against his chest protectively and whispered against my ear, "Even with your description, I do not know what he looks like."

I sighed, frustrated. "Don't bother looking. I don't see him, either now." I closed my eyes and blew out a breath, feeling like I was beginning to lose my mind. Until that moment, I had managed to not think of Ross. I again sighed deeply. "I must have just imagined it."

Sergei again said nothing, but I sensed his worry for me. I felt his embrace tighten, and for the moment, the safety of his arms was enough to calm my fears a little.

The following day after we shared tearful goodbyes with Sergei's family, he decided to cheer me up by taking me for a drive through the country. He knew how much I was going to miss them and he promised me he would take me to see them soon.

I always loved driving through the countryside. From a distance I admired the endless rolling hills and thick clusters of trees. The houses and cottages dotting the hillsides gave the land a look of enchantment.

At one point, we turned on to a gravel road leading over a grassy knoll. When we reached the bottom I smiled as my eyes fell on a large pond.

Sergei pulled over and parked. When we got out, he opened the trunk and took out a blanket. Then he took my hand and led me down to the edge of the pond. We spread the blanket out and sat down, stretching our legs out in front of us.

"This is beautiful," I said, watching a family of ducks approaching from the far side of the pond.

"It is," Sergei agreed.

"John used to take me fishing at a spot that looked similar to this in Knoxville. We'd pack a lunch and stay there for half the day with our poles in the water." I paused, smiling at the memory. "Sometimes we'd talk, sometimes we just sat in silence." I chuckled. "He had the hardest time trying to teach me how to bait my own hook."

Sergei laughed. "Were you afraid of worms?"

"No, it wasn't that. My problem was trying to get the whole worm on without breaking it in half. When that happened, the inside of the worm was usually all over the outside, and he couldn't get me to touch it after that. He'd just

107

pull out a fresh worm for me and hope I was successful in not decapitating it."

"I am guessing John learned a lot of patience taking you fishing," he said chuckling.

"He did." "But I guess it was just important to have that time together." I again smiled at the memory. "He made time for his girls, too, but looking back, I think our time together was special because he knew I needed it most."

Sergei pressed a gentle hand to my face. "I'm sure it was," he said softly. He looked out across the water and sighed, becoming thoughtful. "I learned to skate on a pond this size. I was about six."

I smiled. "Was it hard to learn?"

"Not for me." He smiled fondly. "From the moment my father put the first pair of skates on my feet, I was hooked. And I had not even gotten on the ice yet. Still, I knew I would love it."

"I've never been ice skating, not even roller blading."

His brows lifted. "Never?"

I shook my head and smiled. "I think I was always too afraid to try it. I was scared of falling and breaking something, but I did enjoy watching other people skate."

Sergei's sensuous mouth turned up in a wide grin. "Oh, angel, we will have to do something about that."

I covered my eyes and groaned. "I knew you were going

to say that."

He pulled me close and laughed. "It will be fun, you will see."

"Well, as long as you will be there to break my fall."

He smiled and said, "I will even let you fall on me, all right?" When I raised a brow seductively, he laughed and lay back, pulling me down for a kiss. As we slowly became lost in each other, the subject was forgotten.

But bright and early the next morning, Sergei announced that we were going shopping for both in-line skates and ice skates for me. When I groaned again, he again silenced me with his kiss and told me it would be fun.

Later that morning as Sergei began leading me around our large circular driveway, I laughed, not able to believe I was actually on a pair of skates. Of course, the way he padded me up made me feel like I was about to compete in a full contact sport, but it was fun learning. And he was a good teacher. Most of the time he stayed in front of me, holding my hands and skating backwards, trying to help me keep my balance. Each time he let go for a few seconds and I was able to continue a little on my own, he would take my hands in his again and reward me with a kiss. That alone was worth the effort.

A half an hour later Sergei declared that he'd had enough, but I kept going for a little while longer, having gotten so much better that I didn't want to quit. Sergei sat on the grass and watched me, a smile lighting his handsome face. After another while, he laughed and declared he had created a monster. I laughed, feeling giddy inside over my accomplishment. I had come so far, and I was now willing to try things I had always been too scared to try before. With Sergei, I felt like I could do anything.

The next week he took me ice-skating and I had even more fun. It felt wonderful having his arm around me as we skated around the rink together. When it came to being on the ice, I felt safer having him beside me, but I was still brave enough to go out alone, just as long as there was a guard rail nearby.

To reward me for all my hard work, Sergei treated me to a banana split afterwards. He said he was proud of me for being brave enough to do it. I told him if I was brave, it was because of him. He smiled and kissed me. And I knew that as long as he was by my side, nothing would ever be impossible. With him, I could face anything.

Downtown Stockholm

Ross turned the vodka bottle up and took a healthy swallow, then another and plotted the second phase of his plan. His cell phone continually buzzed with texts and voice mail messages from his parents. Somehow they had found out about his trip and were trying to reach him and talk him into coming back. His mother had even suggested counseling the week before, maybe even checking him into a high-class treatment facility. He hung up on her and hadn't answered his phone since.

He silently watched people coming in and going out of the bar. His eyes moved to a couple in the corner. The two were drunk and all over each other. He despised loose women. As far as he was concerned, they were only good for one thing, and each time he used one for that one thing he hated her for it afterward. There was only one woman in the world worth having, only one woman he deemed worthy of his affections, and he was about to get her back and make the man who dared to put his hands on her pay for touching her.

Yeah, she would be in his arms again soon enough, and she would give him the love and respect he deserved, whether she wanted to or not.

Sixteen

It was on the anniversary of our second month of marriage that it happened. And like the violence of a tornado, it came without warning, turning my world upside down and leaving me to wonder if I would ever be able to piece it back together again.

I had spent the morning cleaning the house, and most of the afternoon packing. We'd surprised Oksana and Nikolai a couple of days before when we called them and told them we were coming to visit them for a week. I looked forward with anticipation to visiting the country of my husband's birth, and I was excited to see his family again. Sergei was excited as well.

He told me about all the places he wanted to show me when we got there. I looked forward to seeing the famous Red Square and touring The Kremlin and St. Basil's Cathedral. Until marrying Sergei, I'd never had a desire to visit Russia. I was sure this was going to prove to be an educational experience.

After we finished packing, Sergei surprised me by putting together a picnic dinner for us. He kept my hand in his as we walked down to the harbor. We spread a blanket out on a grassy knoll and lay on our backs, taking in the sounds that surrounded us.

At one point we laughed as the cry of the seagulls seemed to compete with the loud hum of the boat engines. Then as quickly as the two sounds came, they were gone, leaving the soothing sound of waves lightly lapping against the shore.

Sergei turned to me and smiled, gently cupping my face with his warm hand. "Have I told you how much I love you?"

I smiled back, covering his hand with mine. "Yes, my love, you have."

"Well, he said, pulling me closer, "Have I told you how happy you have made me?"

I nodded, tears slowly filling my eyes. "You not only tell me those things every day, you show me too." I caressed his lips softly. "Have I told you how much I love you, and how happy you have made me?"

He pressed my fingers to his lips, kissing them lightly.

"Every day," he said softly. He gazed at me a moment longer and asked in a raspy voice, "Are you really hungry right now?"

I shook my head with a smile, warmed by the look in his eyes.

"Neither am I." He stood and held out a hand to me. I took it and he pulled me up. Looking longingly into each other's eyes, we picked up the picnic basket and blanket and quickly walked back to the house.

Neither of us wanted to get back out of bed, so we decided to turn in early. Sergei laughed and joked about how lazy we had both become. I told him I enjoyed being lazy with him and he echoed my sentiments.

After a while, the warmth of my husband's arms combined with the blissful memories of all we'd shared that day filled my thoughts and slowly lulled me to sleep.

I hadn't been asleep long when the telephone rang. I turned over and glanced at the clock, wondering who would be calling, but when the time finally registered in my mind, I realized it wasn't really that late.

"*Hej*," I answered slightly groggy. My greeting was met with silence. "Hello," I said once more.

"You shouldn't have left me, honey."

Upon hearing the sound of the voice, I pressed a hand to my pounding heart and literally felt the blood drain from my face. "How did you get this number?" My voice and body were suddenly alert and I was shaking with fear.

By now Sergei had awakened fully and was sitting up. I gripped his arm tightly, moved the phone away slightly and whispered, "It's Ross."

Sergei swore softly and grabbed my hand.

"What do you want?" I asked, trying to sound calm.

"You know what I want."

"Listen," I said, trying to keep my voice from cracking, "I'm married now, so please leave me in peace."

"I'll never leave you in peace because you belong to me. And you're going to pay for giving him what is supposed to be mine."

"I don't belong to you!" I cried loudly. "I'll never belong to you!" When I became too emotional to speak, Sergei angrily took the phone.

"Listen," he said in a heated voice, "I do not know what your problem is, but you *will* stop harassing my wife. Do not ever call here again. And if you ever come near her, you will wish you had not." He hung up and immediately pulled me to him.

Unable to hold back any longer, I buried my face against his chest and sobbed. I was so afraid, I didn't know what to do.

Sergei held me tightly to him and whispered words of comfort, but I could still hear the subtle anger in his voice

"He's going to come after me," I said when I was finally able to stop crying enough to speak. "I know he will."

"Shhh, angel. I am here, and I will never let him hurt you."

"Oh, Sergei," I cried against his chest, "what are we going to do? I can't live like this, always worrying and wondering if or when he will show up."

"Shhh," he soothed once more. "Everything will be all right. I promise."

I closed my eyes and hiccuped, trying not to cry anymore. I wanted to believe him. I *needed* to believe him, but I couldn't help thinking that my nightmare was about to come true. Since Ross now had our number, I knew it was only a matter of time before he found our home. The thought of him being anywhere near our house sent chills through me.

Sergei continued to hold me close. He gently caressed my hair over and over while I silently repeated the same prayer again and again—that we would be safe. But though my heart began to calm a little, I still felt tense. My safe world no longer felt safe.

"Try to get some sleep, angel," Sergei whispered.

I sighed and pressed my face to his chest. "I don't know if I can."

"I will keep you safe," he whispered soothingly into my hair.

Listening to his calm heartbeat and the assuring tone in his voice, I slowly began to relax.

Sometime later, the sound of shattered glass jarred us both awake. I clutched Sergei's arm, fear taking hold of me all over again.

"What is it?" I whispered, my voice shaky.

"I don't know," he answered, gripping my hand. Without turning the light on, he got up.

I held on to his hand panicking. "What are you going to do? Don't go out there," I pleaded.

"I am not," he said, trying to calm my fears.

He quickly moved through the room in the darkness. He went into the closet and took something down from the shelf. Five seconds later he came back out, loading a gun and my heart threatened to pound right through my chest. I had always known the gun was there, but I prayed we would never need to use it.

As the moon inched over the skylight and brightened the room a little, Sergei quietly went over and locked the bedroom door.

"I'm so scared," I whispered. When he came back over to me and took my shaking body in his arms, I clung to him, again praying that my nightmares weren't about to come true.

"If it is him, I will not let him hurt you, Heaven," Sergei whispered vehemently against my brow. "We will be fine."

Just as my heart began to calm a little, I heard footsteps on the stairs and I burrowed further into his chest, completely terrified. A minute later there was a noise outside our bedroom door.

"Come on out here, Heaven," Ross' voice called through the door. The sound of it made my blood run cold.

Sergei quickly pushed me behind him. By now the gun was loaded and he had it aimed at the door. "Go into the bathroom!" he whispered frantically.

"I don't want to leave you!" I cried. "He'll kill you! I know he will!"

"I will be fine!" he hissed. "Get in the bathroom!"

"Come on, Heaven!" Ross called again, banging against the door. "I told you I would find you. If you come out, I'll let him live!"

I turned and looked at Sergei, now more fearful for his life than mine. "*Serioque . . .*"

"*Nyet!*" he hissed, reading my thoughts in my terrified expression. He squeezed my hand tightly. "Get in the bathroom, Heaven. Lock the door."

I finally nodded, my lips trembling as he tore his hand from mine and pushed me toward the bathroom.

In that next instant, the door was kicked open. An ear-piercing scream ripped from my throat as two shots were immediately fired. Then, I watched in slow motion as Ross' shadowed body fell to the floor.

Sergei turned to me in the darkness, gripping my arm. "Are you all right?" he asked, his breathing slightly labored.

I nodded my head, still too shocked to speak. Sergei released me, then moved back and turn on the overhead light. I pressed my hands to my mouth as my eyes took in Ross' body lying face down in a pool of blood, his head slightly turned to the side. Now that I was actually seeing him, I knew for sure that my mind hadn't been playing tricks on me that day in town. I really had seen him in the crowd. Thankfully, after tonight, I would never have to see him again.

Hearing a bump behind me, I turned and immediately cried out in horror as Sergei fell to the floor. The front of his chest was completely covered in blood.

"Sergei!" I screamed, kneeling down beside him, crying profusely. "Oh, Sergei, no! Please no! Sergei!" I cried his name again

He shook his head slightly and tried to speak, but no sound came. He struggled to keep his eyes opened but failed and they soon closed and he lost consciousness.

119

Trying to calm my anguish enough to think, I put two shaky fingers to his neck to check for a pulse. It was weak, but it was there.

Forcing myself to move, I called for an ambulance. I was crying so hard, I could barely talk to give them our address. When they said someone would be right out, I slammed the phone down and went back to Sergei.

I sat with his hand in mine, sobbing and praying with all my heart that the paramedics would get there in time. I knew if I lost him now, my life would be nothing. There would be no way I could go on without him.

Seventeen

The present

Pressing the back of my husband's hand against my face, I glance at the clock again. The sun came up hours ago and the breakfast that had been brought in for me was now cold. I have no desire to eat, but the nausea I am now experiencing forces me to pull the tray table over and take a few bites.

Feeling my stomach calm some, I push the rest of the food away and again take Sergei's hand in mine. I press my free hand against my abdomen and smiled sadly. Having experienced nausea the morning before as well, and with my period being two weeks late, I know what the prognosis will be. I wish I could share my speculation with my husband. I pray with all my heart I will still have the chance.

Still holding onto Sergei's hand, I press my head into my other one and close my eyes, grateful the whole ordeal is finally over. Ross is gone now, and he will never be able to hurt anyone again. That knowledge is a relief. Even still, there is indescribable pain left in his wake.

The questioning I had gone through by the police had been thorough but quick. There was no question Sergei had shot Ross in self defense. And I wasn't surprised to find out Ross already had an assault record. He just seemed to go from bad to worse. Now he was gone, period. And for that, I am extremely grateful. Now if I could just get out of the habit of being afraid. I have feared him for so long, I don't know how *not* to be afraid. I will work on it, though, and I will be better.

My thoughts shift to my grandparents. When I called them and told them what happened, they said they would call Oksana and Nikolai for me. As emotional as I was, I knew I couldn't have called, and I was very grateful for their willingness to do it.

Hearing the door open, I wearily look up as the doctor entered. Fortunately for me, he is American, so I don't have to deal with the language barrier. I watch and wait quietly, holding my breath as he checks my Sergei for any changes. I have been doing my best to think positively, but my efforts are beginning to wear thin. I pray silently for some good news.

After a few moments, the doctor looks up at me and smiles. "He has improved, Mrs. Petrenko. He is stable now."

I close my burning eyes and lift my face upward, sending a silent prayer of gratitude to the heavens. At last, I feel like I can breathe. I finally feel some semblance of calm, not quite peace yet, but calm.

"Thank you, Doctor," I say, barely masking the emotion in my voice.

He places a comforting hand on my shoulder. "Your husband is very strong. All things considered, his prognosis looks good."

I nod, too overcome with emotion to speak.

"Oh," the doctor says as he opens the door, "your grandparents are out in the hallway waiting for you."

"Thank you," I say. He nods and leaves. I stand and stretch. Gazing at my husband again, I squeeze his hand gently and lean over and kiss his lips softly. "I love you, *Seriozha*," I whisper against his mouth. "And I need you. Please keep fighting and get well. My life is nothing without you." I press my lips firmly to his once more, brushing my hand back through his hair. "I'll be right back, my love." I kiss his hand and lay it by his side, then I go out to my grandparents.

As soon as my grandfather sees me, he opens his arms

and I am comforted by the warmth of his embrace, followed by my grandmother. They both pull back and I can see both questions and worry in their tear-filled eyes.

"He's stable now," I say with a smile. "The doctor says Sergei is strong, and he thinks he'll make it."

They both sigh with relief. I squeeze their hands, grateful beyond words for their support.

My grandfather picks up the tote bag he had placed on the floor. "We brought you a change of clothes."

"Thank you, *Farfar.*"

"I also put some personal things in there for you," my grandmother says. "There are some magazines as well."

I smile. "*Tack, Farmor.*"

"You are welcome," she says, touching my face.

My grandfather places a hand on my shoulder and says quietly, "We are having some people go over today to clean up the place. Everything will be just as it was before when you finally go back."

I blink to clear my vision, sending tears rolling down my face. I embrace him tightly. "Thank you, *Farfar.* You don't know how much I dreaded having to take care of that."

"We can imagine," my grandmother says, wiping my tears. I release my grandfather and embrace her as well. Pulling back she asks, "Can we do anything else for you?"

I shake my head and smile. "You've done more than

enough." I sigh. "How did Oksana and Nikolai take the news?"

"Very hard," my grandmother answers. "They said to tell you they love you and they will be flying in tomorrow afternoon."

I am warmed by the knowledge that they will be coming. I need them very much. "Then it's a good thing everything will be cleaned up."

They nod. "Well," my grandmother says, "we will let you go back to Sergei. Will you call us as soon as anything changes?"

"I will." I embrace them both once more. "Thank you again for everything."

"You're welcome," my grandfather says, kissing my cheek. "We will be praying for him."

I stand for a moment and watch them as they walk down the hall, and I silently thank God for them. Then I go back in to be with my husband.

It is later in the evening and I stand staring out the hospital window. My thoughts are consumed with Sergei and our future. He has shown marked improvement throughout the day and the doctor is now sure he will make a full recovery. But he still hasn't awakened, and I long for that immensely. I ache to be able to look into his beautiful brown eyes, to feel his adoring gaze again warm me, and to hear his soft voice caressing my name, calling me his angel.

I wrap my arms around myself, longing to feel the warmth of his arms. And I ache to share the bit of news that I know will bring him joy. I close my eyes and press my forehead against the cool glass, thinking I will probably need to go home in the morning for a while and prepare for Sergei's family's arrival. But the thought of being away from him even for a moment hurts.

I yawn as exhaustion begins to catch up with me, but I know sleep will be slow in coming again. I also know I need to force myself to rest, especially now. Deciding that I will at least try tonight, I heave a quiet sigh and take in the sight of the sun slowly fading into the horizon. The view is causing a feeling of peace to slowly settle around me. In fact, I am so absorbed in its calming effect that I am startled to hear my beloved Sergei's voice weakly calling my name.

I turn from the window and quickly go to him. "I'm here, *Seriozha*," I say, sitting down on the side of the bed, taking his hand in mine, and pressing it against my now wet face. The joy and relief that surges through me upon hearing his gentle voice is indescribable.

Sergei slowly opens his eyes and looks at me. His hand tightens around mine gently. He loosens one finger and brushes a tear away from my face. Then he smiles and his eyes fill with tears. "I love you, *dushenka* . . . and I will always keep you safe."

I lean down and press my head into the pillow next to his and cry. My heart is filled with gratitude for his life. Feeling his other hand softly caressing my hair, I cry even more. After a few moments, I raise slightly and look down into his face. "I love you so much, Sergei. I was so afraid that I was going to lose you." My voice cracks. "I'm so sorry about everything."

He lightly touches my face. "There is nothing for you to be sorry for." He lets his thumb caress my lips. "As for me, I am not going anywhere." He moves his hand to the back of my head and gently pulls me down, urging my lips to his. I sigh as I feel his warm mouth soften under mine, and I am surprised by the strength and intensity of his kiss. It is as if he has only awakened from a night's sleep and is pulling me close for our usual morning kiss.

As if he is reading my mind, he releases my mouth and whispers, "I will never let a day pass without experiencing that."

I smile and fresh tears fill my eyes. "I'll hold you to that." I sit back and wipe my eyes, keeping his hand in mine. "How are you feeling? Are you in pain?"

"Some, but I will live."

I smile and kiss his hand. "Yes, you will. That's the important thing."

127

He brings my hand to his face and looks at me intently. "It is all over now, Heaven. You do not ever have to be afraid again."

I caress his face and sniff as more tears come. "I know. I'm grateful to God for sending you to me."

"Ah, angel," he whispers, "It was you who was sent to me. I prayed, and you came into my life right when I needed you."

I smile again and my heart is full of happiness. I take his hand and slowly move it to my stomach, holding it there. "God is sending you someone else as well." There is a look of question in his eyes. When I smile tearfully and nod, his look changes to one of amazement. His trembling lips curve up into a smile as tears roll back into his hair. I lean down and kiss the tears from his face

Taking my face in his hands and guiding my lips to his to bless me with the warmth of his kiss once more, he sums it up with one whispered statement that will forever ring true in my heart.

"He sent me another little piece of heaven, so earth just keeps getting better."

Eighteen

Sergei

Sergei is in pain, but he says nothing. He will not interrupt this beautiful moment he is sharing with his wife, so he keeps silent until the doctor or nurse comes. He closes his eyes and continues to soak in her warmth.

He had promised to keep Heaven safe, and he had kept that promise. She is safe now. Ross is dead at his hand. He feels remorse over taking a life, but he would do it again to protect his wife. The painful bullet hole in his chest is no great sacrifice to him. He would give his blood and more for her.

He thinks back to the first time he opened the door and

saw Heaven. He remembers the guarded look in her eyes, the vulnerability her exquisite face expressed, but he also remembers the strength that radiated from her. Having been told ahead of time by her grandparents what she had been through, that strength won him over and she captured his heart that very day, and he knew he would never get it back. Even still, he had been determined not to push her in any way. He would simply be a friend to her because he knew that was what she'd needed.

God had then smiled on him through that friendship and had soon blessed him with the gift of her love.

He pulls his thoughts back to the present. He moves his hand down and presses it against Heaven's flat stomach. She draws back slightly and he looks into her beautiful eyes and smiles. His heart is singing because his child is growing inside her, and he is now experiencing the ultimate feeling of peace. His eyes trail over her face and his lips follow. Holding her close and pressing his face into her hair, he closes his eyes and offers a prayer of gratitude to the heavens for the life he has been given, for the gift he is holding in his arms, for the privilege he has had of drying Heaven's tears and offering her comfort, for the future blessings that will come from loving her and making her smile. He has one goal in his heart, a goal he will do everything in his power to fulfill—to make sure the tears of Heaven will never again be ones of sadness—they would only be ones of joy.

Epilogue

Almost a year later.

I sit on the sofa in the family room with Sergei's arms wrapped around me as we gaze down at the sleeping little boy in my arms. I smile contentedly as little Nikolai stretches his chubby little arms and yawns softly.

"I can't believe how big he is getting," Sergei says, touching his soft cheek.

I smile up at him. "I know. It seems like only yesterday we brought him home. At the rate he eats, he will be as big as a toddler before he's even six months old."

Sergei laughs. "My mother says he is taking after me. I

was also nine pounds when I was born."

"So," I say teasing, "I have you to blame for our baby's giant genes, huh?"

"I am afraid so."

"Well," I say, pressing a hand to his face, "considering how amazing his father is, I hope our Nikolai continues to take after you." Sergei leans down and kisses me warmly and I add, "Nothing would make me happier."

As he rests his lips against my brow, I close my eyes and I offer up another prayer of gratitude for my life. Looking back on my life and remembering the rejection and pain I had felt when I was younger, I'd had no clue of the path it would take.

As I think about the painful experiences of my youth, as well as part of my adulthood, and then think about the love that interceded with each experience, I am filled with renewed awe. Because I really do have a reason for being here. My life does have a purpose, and I really am worthy of being loved. And that knowledge most of all, is what brings me the most joy.

Yes, God had known what was best for me after all.

About the Author

J. (Jewel) Adams stays crazy busy with her family and writing. She has written several books in different genres and is also a motivational speaker to both youth and adult audiences. She home schools her four kids that are still at home, and between that and conjuring up new ideas for her books, her brain is completely fried most of the time. She and her husband Sean are the parents of eight children, which means they are both losing hair, but hey, that's what Rogaine is for, right?

In her spare time (when she has any) she likes to curl up with a good book and a healthy stash of orange Tic Tacs. She and her family reside in Utah.

Jewel loves hearing from her fans, so if you would like to contact her to tell her how much you love her books or give her sympathy for the fried brain, or suggestions for the hair loss problem (for her husband, of course) contact her at **jewela40@gmail.com**

Also visit her website and blog at **jadamsnovels.com** and **jewelsbestgems.blogspot.com**

Books by J. Adams/Jewel Adams

The Journey – YA Fantasy

Against the Odds – Contemporary Romance

Mercedes' Mountain – Contemporary Romance

E-books

The Wishing Hour – Romantic Sci-Fi Fantasy

Of Blessings and Dreams: The Legacy – LDS Contemporary Romance

Tears of Heaven – LDS Contemporary Romance

Place In This World: The Sequel to The Journey – YA

Fantasy

The Journey – YA Fantasy

For Love of Angel – YA Romance

Elise's Heart – YA Romance